A SNOWY LITTLE CHRISTMAS

LAYLAH ROBERTS

Laylah Roberts

A Snowy Little Christmas

© 2022, Laylah Roberts

laylahroberts.com

ALL RIGHTS RESERVED. This book contains material protected under International and Federal Copyright Laws and Treaties. Any unauthorized reprint or use of this material is prohibited. No part of this book may be reproduced or transmitted in any form or by any means, electronic or mechanical, including photocopying, recording, or by any information storage and retrieval system without express written permission from the author/publisher.

Cover Design by: Allycat's Creations

Editing: Woncas Creative

Photographer: Golden Czermak

Cover Model: Michael Scanlon

❀ Created with Vellum

LET'S KEEP IN TOUCH!

Don't miss a new release, sign up to my newsletter for sneak peeks, deleted scenes, and giveaways:
https://landing.mailerlite.com/webforms/landing/p7l6g0

You can also join my Facebook readers group here:
https://www.facebook.com/groups/386830425069911/

BOOKS BY LAYLAH ROBERTS

Doms of Decadence

Just for You, Sir

Forever Yours, Sir

For the Love of Sir

Sinfully Yours, Sir

Make me, Sir

A Taste of Sir

To Save Sir

Sir's Redemption

Reveal Me, Sir

Montana Daddies

Daddy Bear

Daddy's Little Darling

Daddy's Naughty Darling Novella

Daddy's Sweet Girl

Daddy's Lost Love

A Montana Daddies Christmas

Daring Daddy

Warrior Daddy

Daddy's Angel

Heal Me, Daddy

Daddy in Cowboy Boots

A Little Christmas Cheer

Sheriff Daddy

Her Daddies' Saving Grace

Rogue Daddy

A Little Winter Wonderland

Daddy's Sassy Sweetheart

MC Daddies

Motorcycle Daddy

Hero Daddy

Protector Daddy

Untamed Daddy

Her Daddy's Jewel

Fierce Daddy

Savage Daddy

Boss Daddy

Daddy Fox

A Snowy Little Christmas

Harem of Daddies

Ruled by her Daddies

Claimed by her Daddies

Stolen by her Daddies

Haven, Texas Series

Lila's Loves

Laken's Surrender

Saving Savannah

Molly's Man

Saxon's Soul

Mastered by Malone

How West was Won

Cole's Mistake

Jardin's Gamble

Romanced by the Malones

Twice the Malone

Mending a Malone

New Orleans Malones

Damaged Princess

Vengeful Commander

Men of Orion

Worlds Apart

Cavan Gang

Rectify

Redemption

Redemption Valley

Audra's Awakening

Old-Fashioned Series

An Old-Fashioned Man

Two Old-Fashioned Men

Her Old-Fashioned Husband

Her Old-Fashioned Boss

His Old-Fashioned Love

An Old-Fashioned Christmas

Bad Boys of Wildeside

Wilde

Sinclair

Luke

Standalones

Their Christmas Baby

A Cozy Little Christmas

Haley Chronicles

Ally and Jake

1

F*ox, Brody, and Autumn*

"Watch out, Brody-bear, I'm coming down!"

Brody turned at the bottom of the stairs, alarm filling his face. "Tutu, what are you doing?"

"I'm going to toboggan down the stairs. Since there's no snow yet, I figured this is the closest I'm going to get to tobogganing." She was already sitting on the toboggan, which was poised on the edge of the top stair. One hand held the toboggan, while the other one was wrapped around a spindle of the staircase.

"No, no, no, it's not safe!" Brody cried.

"Pfft! I'm wearing my helmet." She was quite proud of herself for remembering to put her helmet on. "So my noggin is going to be safe while I ride my toboggan. Oh wow. Listen to me, I could be a poet. Maybe that's my true calling. I thought it was to be a ballerina or a hairdresser. I mean, it could be if you guys would let me get some practice. You won't even let me touch your hair."

"You turned my hair blue!" he protested.

"Yeah, and you looked sick."

"I looked sick? Did it make me look pale?" he asked. "Do I look sick now? Shoot, if the Fox comes home and sees me looking ill, I'm going to find myself in bed for the next month."

"No, you don't look ill, silly. Sick is a word that the kids use nowadays. It means cool."

"Ahh, Tutu, pretty sure that sick isn't a word that kids use."

"Sure it is. You just have to be a cool kid. Like me." She pointed at herself. Unfortunately, she'd used the hand that had been holding onto stairs. The toboggan wobbled underneath her as she cried out. "Brody!"

"It's okay! I'm coming. Lean back."

"I can't!" she cried as the toboggan started moving down the stairs. Her entire body rattled. It felt like her teeth were going to fall right out of her gums as she flew down the stairs.

"Brody! Get out of the way!"

Brody dove to the side as she reached the bottom, falling off the toboggan onto her side. She rolled onto her back, trying to catch her breath.

Whoa.

Had that really just happened?

"Tutu? Tutu! Are you all right?" Brody's worried face appeared above her. "Are you hurt? Did you hit your head? Are you bruised?"

She tried to take a deep breath to answer him, but her heart was racing, and she was still slightly winded.

"That was . . . awesome!"

"Awesome? Awesome!" His eyes widened. "It was not awesome, Tutu! You could have been seriously hurt. Oh my God, Papa is going to kill us!"

Poor Brody. He was so stressed that he was regressing.

"He won't . . . kill us . . . just me . . ."

"Nuh-uh, we're both dead meat when he gets home. When he's not here, I'm in charge." Brody crouched down next to her.

"That's silly," she said. "You can't be in charge of me. We're a triangle. And you're a Little too."

"I'm a Middle. That means I have seniority. Darn it, Tutu. You could have gotten hurt! What were you thinking?"

She tried to sit up. Ouch. She really did hurt all over. Brody helped her sit.

"Tutu, are you sure you're okay?" he asked. "Do I need to get you to the doctor?"

"How would you do that?"

"I dunno. Maybe I'd drive you."

"You would? But we're not allowed to leave the den without permission. And you don't like to drive." Brody was usually a rule follower. She tried to follow the rules . . . mostly. She was a good girl, but also, she liked to experiment.

Only, Daddy had told her no experiments when he wasn't around. Her last experiment had nearly blown up her house.

Mild exaggeration, but otherwise a true story.

But this wasn't a dangerous experiment . . . well, other than the fact that she could have hit her head and knocked herself out. Or broke something . . . like her neck.

"I'd do it for you."

"I'm okay, really." She chewed her lower lip. "Only, Daddy is gonna whip my butt, isn't he?"

"Oh, yep. He totally is." Brody sat on the floor and she climbed onto his lap. Ouch, her body was feeling the effects of being bounced around. "But my butt is in trouble too."

"How come, Brody-bear? You didn't do anything wrong."

"Have you seen the time?" Brody turned his wristwatch around. It was a *Spiderman* watch, and it was so cool. She had a cherry watch. And both watches told her that it was nearly one in the morning.

Uh-oh.

She unzipped the front pocket of her onesie and drew Freddy Fox out from his little pouch. Then, sliding a thumb into her mouth, she leaned against Brody's chest and sucked on it.

"I suppose we should go to bed now," Brody said.

But she didn't want to go to sleep. She was worried about the Fox, and she knew Brody-bear was too. In the four months since the Fox declared that he was retiring, he'd rarely left the den without them.

And he wasn't supposed to be taking on any jobs. But he'd gotten a lead on a guy who'd been a regular at the auctions. Someone who'd bought several women. And he hadn't been able to resist doing a bit of research. Brody had even helped with some of that.

Still . . . while she understood he wouldn't be around all the time, it was hard to wait at home when he could be in danger.

Brody rubbed his hand up and down her back. "He's fine, Tutu. He texted to say he'd be coming home late."

"I know," she mumbled around the thumb in her mouth. Freddy Fox was held tight in her other hand. "He's the Fox. He's invincible. But sometimes, I worry."

"Is that why you thought you'd toboggan down the stairs? Because you were worried?"

"And cause it's a week out from Thanksgiving and there's no snow! I want to toboggan on the snow, but where is it?"

"I don't know if Papa will let you get on a toboggan again, Tutu," Brody told her in a soft voice.

"I didn't get hurt, Brody-bear," she protested.

"But you could have," he countered, running his hand over her hair. "Don't you know how precious you are to us?"

"You're precious to us, too." She never wanted him to feel

anything but completely wanted and desired.

She stared up at him, watching as his cheeks grew red.

"I know."

"Do you know how much we love you?" She started tickling him.

"Uh-huh. No, stop!"

He started giggling as she moved her fingers over all his ticklish spots. He slid onto his back, wriggling around as she straddled his hips, working her magic.

"Tutu, no! Enough! I'll pee my pants."

She stopped, then put her hands on the floor on either side of his head. "I love you, Brody-bear."

Reaching up, he drew her down toward him, kissing her gently. "I love you too, my Tutu. Beautiful girl."

It was her turn to blush.

He sat up suddenly and clasped her face between his hands. "But you still deserve a spanking for what you just did."

She pouted. "Do we have to tell Daddy? I mean . . . if we put the toboggan away, he never has to know."

Brody just eyed her. "Really? You want to hide this from our assassin Daddy? He probably just got a chill on the back of his neck and is driving his Foxmobile here at full speed."

She laughed. "He doesn't have a Foxmobile."

"That we know of. That man has so many vehicles, there could be one hidden back there."

"Ooh, or we could get him one for Christmas. He's impossible to buy for."

"That would be hilarious. Except, he couldn't really drive it anywhere. That would be advertising who he is."

"Huh, true. What about a toy one? A special one, like those figurines you have but never play with. Which I still don't get."

"Because they're worth money in the box."

"So you plan on selling them one day?" she asked.

"Never! I'll die with them. They'll be buried with me."

She stared at him in shock.

He gave her a sheepish look. "Well, you and the Fox too, of course."

"We're gonna need a massive coffin." She shuddered. "Actually, let's not talk about it. I don't wanna die."

Brody gathered her close, holding her tight. She sighed, letting him settle her. She always felt better with one of her men near. But it was even better with both of them close by, touching her.

"I don't think Papa would let you toboggan, even if this hadn't happened. At least not on your own."

"Why not? I'm a fantastic tobogganer. I reckon I could have been in the Olympics, I'm that fast. Did you not see me hold on?"

"Oh yeah, you were holding on for dear life. I saw my life flash before my eyes. Please don't do that again, Tutu. I don't think my blood pressure can take it. Do I have any new gray hairs?"

"What are you talking about?" she asked, trying to tame his wild hair with her fingers. "You never had any gray hairs."

"Sure I did. I got them after you dyed my hair blue."

"I told you, there must have been some fault in the dye. I followed the instructions exactly. Besides, I thought you looked cute with blue hair."

"I looked like a giant Smurf."

"Do Smurfs have blue hair? If your skin was blue, then you'd be a Smurf."

"My skin was blue! My face went blue from the dye."

"Oh, yeah," she drawled slowly. "You looked so adorable. Like having my own giant Smurf."

He shot her a quelling look. "You are never dyeing my hair again."

"Fine. I mean . . . I was only practicing anyway. Your hair is perfect the way it is. But maybe we could do a bit of a cut. It's getting kind of long."

"No. No way, Tutu. Do not even think about it."

Her bottom lip dropped out in a pout. "But how am I meant to become a hairdresser if I don't practice?"

"I think you might have to practice on your dolls."

"Ooh, that's not a bad idea. You're so clever, Brody-bear."

"Aww thanks, Tutu. Now, we better get that toboggan upstairs and back into storage."

"Why do you think that Daddy won't let me do any tobogganing? Why buy a toboggan if you're not going to use it? That just seems silly to me," she said as the two of them started carrying it back upstairs to the storage room.

"Well, maybe he'll let you use it if he's sitting behind you. And he's steering."

"But I'm great at steering."

"Uh-huh, I'm sure you are, Tutu."

"Somehow, I think you're doubting me. That's not very nice."

"I'm sorry, Tutu. You're right," he said as they placed the toboggan back into the storage room. He drew her in for a hug.

She leaned against him, feeling exhausted. There had been too much excitement tonight.

"You need to be in bed," he whispered.

"So do you."

"I'm older, I can handle staying up late," the last word was said on a yawn.

"Uh-huh. Sure. Come on, big boy. Let's go to bed."

"I didn't call myself big boy," he protested.

"Didn't you? You should." She winked at him over her shoulder, loving the way he went red. He was such a cutie-pie. "Actually, can I have a drink before bed?"

He frowned slightly. "You don't have to ask, Tutu."

She bit at her lip, moving from foot to foot. "I know . . . I just . . ."

"Oh, you want a bottle? I can make you a bottle."

"Thank you." She dropped her gaze to her feet.

"Hey, Tutu. Look at me."

She glanced up at him and he cupped her face between his hands. "You can always ask me for anything you need, okay? I know I'm not your Daddy, but I will do everything I can to give you whatever you need."

"I don't deserve you, Brody-bear."

"None of that," he said, leaning down to kiss her. "You deserve the world."

Taking hold of her hand, he led her to the kitchen and helped her onto a stool.

"I can gets it, Brody-bear," she said before sticking her thumb into her mouth.

"You just stay there, sweetie. I'll get your bottle. You want it warmed?"

She nodded, pulling her thumb out. "Do you think we can decorate soon? Halloween is already passed. I'm pretty sure that after Halloween is when you're supposed to put up the Christmas tree and stuff."

"I think you're right," he said.

"What do you think Daddy will want to do about Thanksgiving?"

Brody swallowed heavily. "I don't know. He seemed way more interested in going to Thanksgiving at my momma's than I would have thought."

"What do you think they'll make of him?" she asked.

"I think there might be bloodshed. And it might not be his. My sisters are . . ."

"Feisty?" she suggested.

"I was gonna say bloodthirsty Amazon savages, but okay,

we'll go with feisty."

"Brody!" she said, but she grinned. He wasn't really wrong. She'd interacted with them a few times over the phone and they were definitely, um, forceful.

She was more than a little intimidated by them if she was honest. Meeting them at Thanksgiving would be a bit scary. But she knew that deep down, Brody adored them. And it wasn't fair that he couldn't be with them whenever he wanted, especially on holidays.

However, that meant introducing them to the Fox. Because the Fox wouldn't be happy with Brody going on his own, and that definitely posed some problems.

"And then there's the invite from Markovich," Brody said.

They'd all been invited to Markovich's place for Thanksgiving. The Fox was far less interested in taking up that invitation. But in her opinion, that was the one he should consider.

Markovich was his half-brother. He was family.

But he wasn't even considering going there.

Brody shook her bottle, then tested the temperature by putting some on the inside of his wrist.

"Ouch! Ow. Ouchie!"

"Brody-bear!" She jumped off the stool and tried to race toward him, but hit her toe on the island instead.

"Ow! Ouch! Ouchie!" she cried out, grabbing her foot and hopping around.

"Tutu!" Brody called out. "Let me help you!"

"Let me help you!"

They each reached for one another.

"Put your arm under the water," she told him.

"I'll get some ice for your foot," he said.

As they moved in opposite directions, both of them managed to stumble, crying out again.

"What the hell is going on in here?"

2

Fox, Brody, and Autumn

AUTUMN LET OUT A SCREECH, throwing herself at Brody, who somehow managed to catch her without falling over.

Brody glared at the Fox as he held her tight. "Cowbell."

"Fuck. Sorry, Bunny. Are you all right? Did Daddy scare you?" he crooned, reaching for her and lifting her up onto his hip. "What happened?"

"Brody-bear burned himself," she managed to get out.

"What? Where? How?" The Fox set her on the counter and reached for Brody. "Show me, Pup."

"It's barely even a burn," Brody said with clear embarrassment.

The Fox grabbed his chin. "Show me."

Brody blew out a breath. "Fine. See." He held out his wrist. Autumn glanced over at it, wincing at the red spot on his skin.

"Poor Brody-bear. You've got an ouchie. Want me to kiss it and make it better?" she asked.

"Maybe after we've put some cream on it, Bunny," the Fox said.

She nodded and moved closer to Brody while still sitting on the counter. The Fox turned the faucet on, then stood behind Brody, crowding him as he placed his wrist under the water.

"Keep that right there. Don't move. I'm going to get the First-Aid kit."

"I'll keep an eye on him, Daddy. Tutu is on the job."

"Don't think I haven't forgotten that you were limping before," he warned her. He picked up Freddy Fox, who must have gone flying from her hand earlier when she'd hit her toe. He handed him to her, and she held him tight. Then he grabbed a small icepack from the freezer that had a cartoon fox on it. "You just stay on the counter and off your foot." He moved her leg so she was resting sideways on the counter with her foot elevated and placed the ice pack on her toes.

"Aye-aye, Captain Daddy!"

He raised a gray eyebrow. It should be weird, seeing him in disguise. At the moment, he appeared to be a balding man in his fifties with a small pouch of a tummy. Very different from the dark-haired man in his early forties whose abs just didn't quit. But it was like she didn't really notice the disguises anymore.

The Fox eyed her.

"I'll watch her, Papa," Brody said.

He looked back and forth between them. "You're both as bad as each other."

She gasped, insulted. "We are not, Daddy! I'm way worse than Brody-bear." She grinned.

Brody snorted out a laugh. "She is."

"Agreed," the Fox replied. "Just stay put. Anyone who moves gets twice the spanking they're already owed."

"What spanking, Daddy? We been good."

"That so? What time is it, baby girl?"

"I'm not old enough to tell the time, Daddy." She was proud of herself for that comeback. Sometimes, being a Little was the bomb. Hmm, she wondered if the kids were still saying that. She was sure they were because she was just that cool.

The Fox pressed a button on her watch and the time was announced in a robotic voice. "It is one-thirty-three a.m."

"Oh, Brussel sprouts," she muttered.

The Fox just shook his head and disappeared out of the kitchen, muttering something about having to put First-Aid kits in every room. She didn't know why he thought he had to do that. Although, Brody-bear could be a tad clumsy.

She turned her head, peering over at his wrist. "Ouchie, I'm sorry you got hurt making me a bottle." Swinging herself around, her ice pack went flying, but she didn't pay it any attention. She rested her head on his shoulder.

"Hey, it's not your fault, Tutu." He turned and hugged her. "Don't feel bad. It's just a little burn. And it's my fault for making your bottle too hot. Okay?"

"Okay," she agreed. "Quick, best put your wrist back under the water before he comes back. Shoot, where's my ice pack?"

"Here." Brody turned and grabbed it off the floor and she got back into position.

Brody slid his wrist back under the water just as the Fox came into the kitchen. Whew. Just in time. That saved his backside from another spanking. The one he already had coming was going to be bad enough. He clenched his butt cheeks together.

"Now, I know that you didn't disobey me and take your wrist out from under the water, did you, Pup?" the Fox drawled, coming up behind him.

The heat of his body made Brody shiver. He was dressed in a pair of pajama bottoms with candy canes all over them and a black, tight T-shirt. Tutu was wearing a onesie with bears all over it that he'd bought for her. He thought she looked super cute.

"It was my fault, Daddy," Tutu said hastily. "My ice pack went flying."

"All by itself?" the Fox drawled.

"Well, I might have moved a little bit." Tutu gave him a wide smile.

"Hmm, you both just added ten extras to your punishment."

"Fudge knuckles," Tutu muttered.

Ooh, that was a good one. They were both having fun coming up with alternatives to swearing. At least when in Little and Middle headspace.

The Fox reached around and grasped hold of his wrist, just above the burn, and held it more firmly under the icy water.

"Papa, my hand is going to freeze off."

"You'll thank me later. You need to cool that burn off."

Brody was certain it was fine. It didn't hurt. Probably because he couldn't feel his wrist or his hand anymore.

The Fox's nearness was stirring his body. He couldn't help but press his ass back against the other man's crotch, wriggling it back and forth.

"Do you need to go potty, my Pup?" the Fox asked.

He groaned. Part of him wanted to protest the word potty. Another part of him wanted to seize that excuse for the way he'd been moving around.

"I don't need to use the toilet," he admitted.

"No? Then why are you moving around like you have ants in your pants?"

"Maybe you should check he doesn't have ants in his pants, Daddy," Tutu suggested with a wicked grin.

"Excellent suggestion, my Bunny."

She bounced up and down in pleasure.

"I thought so," she replied.

The Fox kept one hand on Brody's wrist while the other traveled down under the waistband of his sweatpants. His hand went around Brody's firm dick, making him groan as he rested his head back on the Fox's chest.

That felt sooo good.

The Fox moved his hand up and down Brody's dick while his breathing grew faster and his pulse raced.

"Good Pup. Do you like that?"

"Yes, Sir."

"I know you do. I can feel how hard you are. Poor Pup, it's going to be hard to sleep with this hard-on."

Brody whimpered. Did that mean he wouldn't get to come?

"Please, Sir," he begged.

"Please what? Let you come? But you've been so naughty and I've got to doctor your wrist."

"My wrist is fine," he protested.

"Uh-uh, Papa will be the judge of that. So I guess your cock will just have to stay hard, your balls aching."

"Ooh, wait! I can help! Pick me! I wanna help!" Tutu was holding her hand up in the air.

Her enthusiasm was killing him. Seriously.

"Hmm, shall I let Bunny play with you?"

"Please, Daddy! Please. I'll be a good girl."

Both Brody and the Fox snorted.

"I'll let you suck on Brody while I deal with his wrist. Wiggle your toes first and show me that they're all right."

The Fox finally turned off the tap. Tutu moved her toes back and forth. "See Daddy, all good!"

"All right, you can help Pup with his little problem."

"Hey!" Brody protested. "It's not a little problem. It's a truly massive problem."

Tutu giggled as the Fox lifted her down.

"Of course it is, Brody-bear," she said loyally. "A huge, enormous, ginormous problem."

"Well, I wouldn't go quite that far," he muttered, his cheeks growing hot.

"Take a step back, Pup," the Fox ordered.

After he stepped back, the Fox threw a clean towel down on the floor in front of Brody's feet.

"There you are, Bunny. Suck our boy off. But, Pup, you're not to come without permission."

Great, so he was about to be tortured.

He held out his hand to Tutu to help her balance as she got down on her knees in front of him. Lord knew they didn't need her hurting herself again.

Or him. Because his family jewels were in a very vulnerable position, and it wouldn't be the first time she'd accidentally kneed him there.

She left Freddy Fox on the bench. Probably just as well. He didn't need to see this.

Reaching up, she drew his pajama pants down as the Fox rummaged through the First-Aid kit. Was he seriously going to deal with the tiny red spot on Brody's wrist while Tutu sucked him off?

She drew his dick into her mouth, sucking vigorously, and Brody groaned.

God. Felt so good.

Why hadn't they done this while they were waiting for the Fox to get home rather than playing video games? Oh, and let's not forget Tutu's tobogganing.

"That feels good, does it?" the Fox asked as he took hold of his wrist once again and dabbed some burn cream on the small spot. This was ridiculous and over-the-top, and it made Brody's heart sing with satisfaction and pleasure.

To know that he was completely and utterly cared for was a blessing and sometimes a curse, depending on how overprotective the Fox was being. He really didn't handle them being hurt or sick at all. Sometimes, Brody thought he was getting worse. The other day, he'd sneezed because of some dust and the Fox had made him spend the entire day in bed.

Yep, the Fox was nuts.

But Brody wouldn't have him any other way.

Tutu moved her mouth up and down his shaft. Then, wrapping her hand around the base of him, she licked her way up his dick before taking him deep once more.

Killing. Him.

He could feel his orgasm growing. It was an ache in the small of his back.

Fuck. He needed to come so badly.

"Please, Sir."

"Please what?" the Fox asked as he wrapped a bandage around his wrist. Was he for real right now?

But before he could ask if that was really necessary, Tutu took him deep and hummed.

Hell's bells.

"I need to come, Sir."

"No, you're not to come yet."

Brody whimpered. This was cruel and unusual punishment. There should be a law against this.

"What if... what if I can't hold it back?"

Tutu drew back and licked the flat of her tongue over the head of his dick.

"You have to hold back until you're given permission." The Fox gripped his chin lightly. "You know what happens if you come without permission, Pup."

Brody swallowed heavily.

The cock cage.

Darn it. Maybe it was worth the punishment of the cock cage if he got to come.

"Don't even think of it, Pup. Because as well as the cock cage, I'll put a vibrating plug in your ass. And I'll have the remote, ready to torture you all day. Is that really worth defying me?" The Fox ran his hand down one ass cheek, squeezing it.

"No, Sir."

"That's right, no. Bunny, keep playing with our boy. I'll be back."

Where was he going? Brody had no idea. He closed his eyes as Tutu took him deep once more.

"Tutu, you have to take it easy on me," he begged. Or he wasn't going to last.

She leaned back, smiling up at him as her hand ran up and down his shaft. "Poor Brody-bear. You need to come really bad, huh?"

"Yes. Darn it. So take it easy on me."

"If you didn't feel so good in my mouth, I might be able to," she said with fake regret.

She was so mean.

"Baby girl, get your mouth back on Pup's dick before I spread you out on the island and have him play with your pussy, edging you until I give you permission to come. Hmm, actually, I might do that anyway."

He whimpered at the same time as Tutu did.

The Fox was now naked. And he'd taken off most of his disguise, Brody realized. The gray hair and eyebrows were still there. But the rest of him was all Fox. Delicious.

The Fox squirted some lube onto his hand, then wrapped his hand around his thick shaft.

Brody licked his lips, wishing he could get his mouth on the Fox's dick.

"Like what you see, Pup? Do you want my dick in your mouth?"

"Yes, Sir."

"Hmm, too bad you've been naughty, huh?" the Fox said. "No good boy treats for you."

Shoot. That shouldn't make his knees go weak. But it did. And it didn't help that Tutu was moving her mouth up and down his dick, sucking strongly. He was so close, he was shaking.

"Please, Sir."

"No, not yet. Don't you come," the Fox warned. "Bend over slightly, spread your legs and put your hands on the counter."

Sugar balls. He was in such trouble here. The Fox parted his ass cheeks and ran a wet finger over his asshole.

"Do you need my cock inside you, Pup?"

"Yes! Please!"

"How much do you need it? Tell me."

"Please, please, so bad," Brody begged as the Fox slid a finger inside him.

There was no way he could hold back his orgasm. He closed his eyes and tried to count backward. Nope, not helpful. He tried to picture his third-grade teacher naked.

Gross. That helped a bit.

"Poor Pup, it's painful, isn't it? Let's see if we can make it all better." By now, the Fox had two fingers inside his ass and was thrusting them back and forth.

"I need to come."

"I know you do," the Fox crooned. "I bet it hurts, doesn't it?"

The bastard didn't sound all that sympathetic. But Brody guessed he wasn't since he was the cause of most of Brody's current problems.

Small whimpers of need and desire escaped him.

"Shh, Pup. You're being such a good boy. Lean over a bit more. That's it. If you keep being a good boy, I'll let you come."

Brody bent over further as the Fox slid his fingers out and slowly replaced them with his dick.

That felt so good. He breathed out, trying to relax and let the Fox slide inside him more easily.

"That's it. Good boy. You feel so good around my dick. What a good Pup you are, taking my cock so well."

Brody groaned as the Fox finally seated himself. It was too much. He could feel how close he was. He needed to come.

"Please. Please. Please."

The Fox grasped his hips, holding him steady before he started to fuck him in earnest.

"Please. Please."

"Please what, Pup? Tell me what you need."

"I need to come. Please! Please, Sir!"

"Then you can come, Pup."

Finally. Thank God for that. He let out a low moan as his orgasm rushed through him. He tried to hold himself steady as the Fox fucked him, not wanting to thrust himself down Tutu's throat. Not that she'd probably mind. She and the Fox had worked up to where she could let him take over and fuck her mouth.

Brody groaned as he came in her mouth. He heard her moan in pleasure. She drew back off his dick, licking it slowly as if she was savoring his taste.

"That was delicious." She grinned up at him.

"What did I ever do to deserve you?" he whispered.

"Think you have that wrong, Brody-bear. It's what did I do to deserve the two of you?"

"I was a fucking saint and was rewarded with the two of you," the Fox told them. "Oh no, wait. I'm the devil and despite my evil ways, I was given the two of you to protect and love. Sometimes the bad guy does win."

Brody frowned, and Autumn climbed to her feet, glaring at the Fox.

"You're not the bad guy, Daddy, and you're not evil. I won't have you saying that. Do I have to spank your butt?" she threatened.

The Fox went still behind him. "You try, baby girl, and I swear you won't sit for a month."

Tutu gulped. "Hmm, I don't think I'll try."

"Good choice," the Fox growled at her. "Bunny, did you like sucking Pup off?"

"Yes, it was soo good. Can I do it again, Daddy?"

Brody groaned. He wouldn't survive.

"Not right now. Maybe later."

"Are you wet?" the Fox asked, sliding in and out of Brody's ass.

"Yes, Foxy," she replied.

"Give me a taste. Prove it."

"H-how?" she asked, staring at him with wide eyes. She was trapped between Brody and the counter, with his arms on either side of her.

"Take your clothes off," the Fox ordered.

Brody watched on as she took her onesie off, standing there naked. Her small breasts were tipped with pink, sweet nipples and his mouth watered.

"Good girl, Bunny," the Fox praised. "Now, I want you to reach down and push your fingers into your pussy. Get them nice and wet."

"Oh dear Lord," she muttered, but she did as ordered, holding up two fingers glistening with her juices.

Brody swore that his mouth was watering. The Fox had stilled inside him, not moving. But he was used to this sort of torture. Sometimes, the Fox liked to make him sit on his lap, nice and still, with his dick deep inside Brody's ass. Every time Brody moved, he'd get an extra minute added on.

Sometimes, he moved on purpose.

"Good girl, now hold them out for me." The Fox leaned forward and took her fingers into his mouth. Brody turned his head to try and watch, but he couldn't get a good view from his position. However, he could hear him sucking on her fingers.

"Delicious," the Fox said. "Do you want a taste, Pup?"

"Yes, please." More than anything. "If that's what Tutu wants."

"Baby girl, get up on the counter, then spread your legs wide. Show Brody just how much you want his mouth on your pussy."

"Yes, Foxy." She moved to the side of the sink and sat on the counter. The Fox shuffled them over so they were still standing in front of her. And then she pushed her thighs wide. Brody licked his lips.

"Make our girl feel good, Brody-bear."

With pleasure.

"Bunny, just so you know, the same rules apply. You're not allowed to come without permission."

"Foxy, that's so mean."

"I know. I'm just a cruel dictator. But it's so much fun. Being in charge is the best."

"I wouldn't know," Brody said mournfully.

"Ooh, pick me!" Tutu said. "I like being in charge."

"And what would you do if you were in charge, Bunny?" the Fox asked.

"I'd make it so you had to let me suck your dicks whenever I wanted. Oh, and that I always got to eat candy."

"The first one we could do. The second is a firm no. Brody, you've been given your orders."

Oh, hell yes.

3

Fox, Brody, and Autumn

AUTUMN LEANED back with her hands on the counter as Brody ran his tongue along her slick lips. She could still taste him on her tongue.

She hadn't been lying when she'd said he was delicious. She'd actually ordered some peppermint-flavored body syrup, which she planned to pour all over his cock.

A Christmas special.

He flicked at her clit and she swore her eyes rolled back in her head. She was already so close just from sucking him off.

Opening her eyes, she stared at the Fox who was fucking Brody with hard, heavy thrusts.

Oh Lord. That was so hot.

She cupped her breast, lightly pinching the nipple. The Fox's gaze zeroed in on her hand as she played with herself.

"Please can I come, Foxy?" she asked pleadingly. She was certain he couldn't say no to her as she gave him wide puppy-dog eyes.

"No, you may not."

She sucked in a sharp breath as Brody flicked her clit with his tongue.

That was just so mean.

She wasn't used to being denied. She wasn't sure she actually could hold off her orgasm.

"Place your hands behind you. Lean back," the Fox ordered. "That's it. Now, push your hips to the edge. Fuck, baby girl. Put your feet on the counter and spread those legs wide."

She whimpered. She was now entirely on display. There wasn't a part of her pussy that Brody couldn't reach. He slid his tongue deep inside her pussy. She moaned. She needed more. To be pushed over the edge. She couldn't handle this for much longer.

"Please, Daddy. Please."

"Not yet."

God. He had to be close, right? And surely he wouldn't leave her hanging. Her whimpers filled the room along with the noises of Brody's ass being fucked. She wished she could see. She loved watching the two of them together.

"Daddy, please!"

"All right, baby girl. You. Can. Come."

She moaned as she found her release. Her head went back as her entire body shuddered. The Fox grunted and she assumed he was coming as well, but she was too busy floating on a cloud of pleasure.

When she came back down to earth, she was aware of the Fox talking in a low voice to Brody, who he had bent over the island. He was wiping him clean with a cloth.

Darn. That was so sexy.

"I can... I can clean myself up, Sir."

"Shh, Pup. You did a good job taking me in your ass while giving our girl an orgasm. Let me take care of you now."

Aww. She loved when the Fox got a bit lovey-dovey.

Hmm, maybe lovey-dovey was the wrong word. The Fox wasn't really the lovey-dovey type.

But he could show a caring side. Even though he'd probably deny it.

"Stand up, Pup. Good boy." Clasping his face with his hand, he kissed Brody hard and hot.

"Jesus help me," Brody muttered.

"Told you that's not going to work." The Fox nipped at Brody's lip. "Put your pajamas back on and wait for me. I've got to get another cloth for our girl."

"I can do it," she said quickly.

"Stay where you are," the Fox ordered her.

"I might have made a mess on the counter."

The Fox snorted. "Messes are my specialty."

Good. Lord.

Her eyes widened as she stared over at Brody. "Do you think he knows what I did?"

"I dunno," Brody said. "Hope not. We're already in trouble for staying up late."

The Fox walked back in with another cloth and moved toward her. There was something in his face that she couldn't read. A sort of knowledge that had a shiver running up her spine.

"Lean back, Bunny. Spread those legs for me."

Swallowing heavily, she did as ordered, moaning slightly at the feel of the warm cloth on the lips of her pussy. He was thorough as he ran the fabric over her.

"Good girl," he told her. "You can sit up now."

He placed his hand around the back of her neck before kissing her.

Oh yum.

When he drew back, she swayed slightly. He lifted her down, then helped her get dressed. She loved it when he took care of her like this.

After handing her Freddy Fox, he picked up the bottle she'd forgotten about. He tipped the ruined milk down the sink.

"Do you want a bottle, baby girl?" he asked gently. "I can make you a new one."

"No, Daddy. Not anymore."

Nodding, he picked her up and settled her on his hip. Then he held his other hand out to Brody. "Come here, Pup."

Brody snuggled in against him.

"Now, that was sick, don't you think?"

She stiffened. Uh-oh. Had she misheard him? She had to have misheard him, right?

That was the only explanation.

"What did you say, Papa?" Brody asked.

"I said wasn't that sick? Isn't that what the cool kids are saying?"

Oh, hell.

Brody met her gaze as she stared at him in shock. There was no way that was a coincidence. There was no such thing as a coincidence with the Fox.

"Hmm, Bunny? Isn't that the word? Sick?"

Crap.

She thought it was fair to say that he not only knew . . . but he wasn't thrilled with her right now. With his hand holding Brody's, he started walking to their bedroom.

"Well, Bunny? Cat got your tongue? Or is it a Fox? Or a bear?"

Oh, heck.

There was no denying it. So she should accept her punishment gracefully—the way she always did.

"Daddy, you can't spank me for it."

"Spank you for what, baby girl?" He took them through the large bedroom and into the attached bathroom. He placed her on the counter between the double sinks.

Then, to her surprise, he turned to Brody and patted the counter on the other side. "Up you go."

"Sir?"

"I'm Papa right now. I think a Little-Middle weekend is in order. Especially with how naughty both of you were tonight . . . well, today since it's now morning. And well past time that a bad Bunny and a naughty Pup were in bed."

"It wasn't Brody-bear's fault, Daddy. I did it all on my own. But don't spank me, Daddy. Pretty please. I'll cry. A lot." She put her hands under her butt, trying to protect it.

Yep, totally accepting her punishment gracefully.

"But I should have been looking after you better," Brody-bear protested.

"It's not your job to watch over me," she argued.

"No, it's mine," the Fox told them firmly. "It's my job to keep the two of you safe. And obviously, I failed."

"So does that mean we get to spank you, Daddy?" she asked.

His brown eyes moved to stare at her. Uh-oh. "What did I say earlier about you spanking me, baby girl?"

"Oh yeah, right."

Silly Autumn.

The big bad Daddy Dom is never going to let you spank him.

Not that she actually wanted to. That would be . . . weird.

"And it's also my job to punish you both when you misbehave."

"I told you, Daddy. It was just me. Not Brody-bear. He's innocent on all charges."

"Is that so?" The Fox turned that glacial gaze on Brody. "What time is your bedtime, Pup?"

"Eleven, Papa."

"What time is it now?" the Fox asked Brody.

"Um, well, it's nearly two in the morning."

"You've both been naughty and tomorrow you'll be punished."

"Tomorrow?" she repeated. "Can't you do it now, Daddy?"

"No. You need sleep."

How easy would it be to sleep with that hanging over them? This was gonna suck. A thought occurred to her.

"So, uh, you can hear us? There's not just cameras?" she asked

"That's right, baby girl. I could hear you talk. I could also see you on the toboggan going down the stairs. Do you know all the things that could have happened to you? You could have broken your neck. You could have knocked yourself out. What would have happened then? What would Brody have done?"

Uh-oh.

He was really, really upset.

"Have you always had that tic there, Daddy?" She pointed next to his right eye.

"No, I have not."

"Oh. Right." Yikes.

"What were you thinking?" he repeated.

Hmm. "I guess I wasn't, Daddy."

"No, you weren't. Both of you will sleep in tomorrow and you can expect a nap as well. After your punishment." He put toothpaste on their toothbrushes. Brody had two. A more adult one and a *Spiderman* one. She just had one with a bunny head on one end. He held them up, one in each hand.

Brody reached for his *Spiderman* one and the Fox gave him a look, pulling it back. "No, you let Papa brush your teeth. Open, both of you."

Autumn was used to it, but she knew Brody was probably struggling slightly. Red tinted his cheeks, but he didn't protest as the Fox brushed their teeth. He was ambidextrous and seemed to do it easily. Then the Fox lifted them off the counter and turned them toward the bedroom.

He slapped their asses. "Get into bed. Now."

Autumn got in on one side and Brody moved to the other, taking off his glasses and setting them on the nightstand. The Fox disappeared had out of the room. She reached into the nightstand drawer and drew out one of her pacifiers. She now had a collection of them. The Fox enjoyed buying her different ones that took his fancy.

Tonight she chose one that had the image of cherries on the front.

When he returned, his disguise was fully gone. He pulled on a pair of pajama bottoms and climbed between them. This was her favorite position to sleep in. With the Fox on his back and both of them curled up on either side of him.

She drew the pacifier from her mouth. "I'm sorry that I was naughty, Daddy."

"I know, baby girl," he said in a low voice.

"We should have gone to bed at our bedtime," Brody-bear added.

"Yes, you should have. And tomorrow, you'll regret that you didn't."

She already regretted that.

"We was worried about you, Daddy."

He ran his hand up and down her back soothingly. "I called you and told you I would be late and to go to bed."

"Yeah, but I was still worried," she told him.

"Me too, Papa," Brody added.

"And I just wanted to do a small experiment to see if tobogganing down the stairs was possible. Spoiler alert. It is."

"I can't have you so worried that you do dangerous things," the Fox said. "Perhaps it's time I looked into hiring you both a nanny."

"What?" She sat up and gaped down at him. "Nuh-uh, Daddy. No nanny!"

"Yeah, we don't need one, Papa!" Brody added, rolling onto his side and leaning up on his elbow.

The Fox stared up at them. "And I want you both safe. If I can't be here, then you might need someone else to watch over you."

"I don't want anyone but you, Daddy!" Trembling, she threw herself into his arms. "I only want you and Brody. I can't . . . I can't have anyone else . . ."

"Hey, shh. Shh, it's all right. No nanny. All right?"

"Tutu, it's all right," Brody-bear told her, rubbing her back. "Papa wouldn't have a stranger here with us, anyway."

No, that's right. He wouldn't.

"Well, she wouldn't be a stranger after a while," the Fox said. "And I'd get someone who was well-trained."

She shuddered at the thought.

"You'd really trust someone you don't know not to tell anyone who you are or where we live?" Brody asked.

"Well, it's not like she'd be able to tell anyone. She'd be stuck here. Forever."

She sat up, staring down at him. "Daddy, you can't kidnap someone and hold them against their will."

"Course I can. It's really quite easy when you know how."

"No, I mean, morally you can't do that, Daddy."

"Morals," he spat out. "I don't bother with those."

She sighed. Silly Daddy.

"And you'd be fine with a stranger touching Tutu? Discipling her?" Brody asked. "You'd trust this stranger?"

"I'd trust no one with he two of you," he said vehemently. "Well, except for my sweet girl, but she's as submissive as the two of you. Fine. Point made. No nanny. Now, the two of you need to get to sleep before my spanking hand starts tingling."

He didn't have to tell her twice. She slammed down on top of him, wondering why he let out a pained groan.

"Is your back sore, Daddy? Or is it your spanking hand? Maybe you shouldn't exert it?"

"It's not his back or his spanking hand," Brody said. "Although she is right when she says you shouldn't exert it, Papa."

"My spanking hand is just fine," the Fox said in a strained voice. "My balls might never be the same again. They're also not little."

"Oh no, why not, Daddy? I love your little ballsy balls. Can I kiss them better?" she asked.

"No!" he said quickly. "No, baby girl. They're fine."

Disappointment filled her, but she yawned and put her pacifier back in her mouth. Seemed weird that he was getting a pain in his balls. Maybe he should have them looked at.

She could offer her services tomorrow.

"Did you find the guy, Papa?" Brody asked.

Oh shoot. She'd forgotten the reason that he'd left them.

"No, it was a false lead. But don't worry, I'll get the bastard."

4

Fox, Brody, and Autumn

"I don't know what all the fuss is about. If they annoy me, then I'll just kill them. Simple. Problem solved."

Turning his head away from the corner he was supposed to be facing, Brody glanced over at the Fox who stood in the middle of the playroom, a frown on his face.

"Well, uh, killing them probably isn't going to make the best first impression, Daddy," Tutu pointed out from her corner.

"And I'd really appreciate it if you didn't hurt them, Papa," Brody added, pushing his glasses up his nose. "Like, really, really."

Really, really? Had he just said that?

"I wouldn't kill them straight away," the Fox explained. "They'd have to annoy me first. I'm not a monster."

"But, Daddy, you can't kill everyone who annoys you," Tutu pointed out.

The Fox folded his arms across his chest, looking mildly curious. "Make your case."

Tutu cleared her throat, turning to face the Fox properly.

"Did I say to move?" he asked smoothly.

"But I can't make my case while facing the corner, Daddy. Besides, I don't think you're gonna punish us anymore."

Brody was tempted to smack his hand against his forehead. What was she thinking, reminding the Fox that he was supposed to be punishing them?

They were facing two separate corners of the playroom. Brody had his gray sweatpants off, his bare ass on display.

Tutu had her tights and tutu down around her ankles and if she didn't stay still she was likely to trip up over them.

She could stumble over air most days. She'd looked so adorable in the tutu that the Fox had bought for her in honor of her nickname. It was pale pink with images of bunnies stitched into it.

Her T-shirt had *Property of The Fox* written along the front.

Subtle the Fox was not. At least not when it came to the two of them and how much he loved them.

Freddy Fox was sitting off to the side, watching everything.

"I'll allow you to turn to make your case," the Fox agreed. "However, I doubt you will sway my mind. I'm usually always right. I'm magnificent like that."

He also wasn't subtle when it came to his feelings about himself. He was happy to tell everyone how amazing he was.

But he wasn't lying. He was amazing. Maybe Brody saw him through rose-colored glasses. A therapist would probably tell him he had Stockholm syndrome or some other syndrome for falling in love with an assassin.

But he hadn't fallen in love with an assassin. He'd fallen in love with a man. A man who might have some quirks, and still might struggle with empathy and emotion.

However, Brody knew he was loved. Autumn was loved. That the Fox would kill for them. Would protect them with everything he had.

Sometimes, it still surprised him that the two of them had chosen to be with him. But he knew better than to voice that thought out loud.

"You can turn as well, Pup, since apparently, you're on Bunny's side."

Uh-oh. Abort.

He shot Tutu a look as he turned around, but she was too busy trying to pull up her tights.

"Did I say you could pull up your tights, Bunny?" the Fox drawled.

"Uh, no, Daddy. But I don't think I can make my case with my hoo-ha showing."

"You can. You will. There's no point putting your clothes when you're going to have to take them back down for your punishment."

Brody gulped.

"But you're not really going to punish us, Daddy," Tutu said confidently.

"I'm not?" The Fox raised an eyebrow. "Why not?"

"Because you'd have done it already. I mean . . . waiting in the corner with our butts on display is really punishment enough."

This time Brody really did slap his hand against his forehead.

"Don't hurt yourself," the Fox growled. "If you need a smack, I'll apply one to your ass for you. But you don't lay hands on yourself."

"Yes, Papa," he said quickly.

The Fox gave him a stern look. "And you'll be getting a spanking soon. I wouldn't go adding to the smacks you're already owed."

No, he didn't want to do that.

"Sorry, Papa."

"Why was you hitting yourself, Brody-bear?" Tutu asked. "Did you see a fly? It wasn't a moth, was it? I don't like moths."

"No, it wasn't a moth or a fly. It just wasn't smart to tell Papa that being in the corner with our butts on display was punishment enough. Now, he'll think we need corner time more often."

"Hmm, I think you're right, Brody-bear" the Fox confirmed. "After Bunny makes her case, I'm going to smack both of your bottoms before I put you down for a nap."

"A nap, Daddy!" Tutu groaned.

"Yes, a nap," the Fox replied sternly. "For both of you." He leveled his gaze at Brody. "You stayed up far too late last night."

"But we lost track of time, Papa."

"Yeah, Daddy," Tutu added. "We didn't realize it was past eleven. You can't blame us for not being able to tell the time."

"You can tell the time. Besides, I set up both of your watches to buzz when it's your bedtime."

"Oh, sugar," Tutu muttered, staring down at the watch on her wrist. The Fox had given them both these watches. They could send and receive texts and calls, there were games on them, and he could use them to track where they were.

They weren't the only GPS trackers they had on them, though. The Fox had put them in every pair of shoes they owned, and stitched them into every piece of clothing. It had taken him hours since he'd done it himself. But he was nothing if not paranoid.

And the watch served as a kind of decoy. Anyone who dared to kidnap them would see the watch and immediately assume that's where a tracker was hidden. Then hopefully not think to check anywhere else.

Not that Brody thought anyone would be able to get to them ever again. Not after Autumn's near kidnapping. The Fox really didn't like them going anywhere and if they had to leave his den, he always accompanied them. And they were under strict instructions to never leave his side. He'd even threatened to leash Tutu since she'd wandered off during their last outing to the toy shop.

Poor Tutu, she'd had her eye on this adorable puppy that walked and pooped and everything and the Fox had made her put it back on the shelf because she'd been naughty.

She'd even got a smack on her ass in the store. No one had seen, but still . . . he'd have been mortified if someone saw him get his butt popped.

Although he was pretty sure that puppy would eventually turn up in the playroom. The Fox spoiled Autumn. Heck, he spoiled both of them. Brody had every video game he'd ever desired as well as so many collectible figurines that it still gave him a shock of pleasure when he walked into his playroom and saw them sitting on the shelves.

Yeah, they were spoiled. Even if the Fox occasionally decided to get all strict on their asses.

"Right, baby girl. Give me your reasons for why I can't just kill anyone that annoys me," the Fox said.

"Oh right, yep. Well, Daddy think of all the dead bodies you'd have to clean up."

"I don't get annoyed that often."

The pair of them shared a look. So naughty. He never really got truly annoyed. Just . . . lightly irritated.

"And that's what a cleaning service is for," he pointed out.

"Yes. But, Daddy, you don't want to be paying their exorbitant prices."

"I have often thought of getting my own crew. But that would involve dealing with people. I don't like people."

"Right . . . but you don't always kill people that annoy you, do you?" she said.

"I don't? Ah, you're talking about those bikers." He sighed. "Yes, I can see how you'd be confused. They annoy me all the time. They're so needy. And they struggle to protect their women, meaning I constantly have to help them. So why don't I take them out? It's a good question and one I've often thought about. And the main reason is that it would upset my sweet girl. I don't want to do that. For some reason she likes them. I mean . . . I'm sure that I could find her someone else, so perhaps you're right and I should get rid of them. It's been a while since I lit a nice fire. Maybe we can turn it into a bonfire. Perhaps roast marshmallows?"

They both stared at him like he'd lost his mind.

The thing was . . . he'd lost it a long time ago. Back in Russia, in an alleyway, when his own flesh and blood ordered him to be beaten. Something in him died that day. Twisted, become warped.

Still, both of them loved roasting marshmallows.

"No marshmallows?" he queried, shocked.

"He's joking, right, Brody-bear?" Autumn asked.

"I . . . can't tell. But yeah, he has to be. There's no way he'd harm the Iron Shadows members. He really does care about them."

He made a scoffing noise. "Fine, yes, I care about them. I won't hurt them." Because it would hurt his sweet girl, his Pup, and his Bunny.

But he had no real attachment to them . . .

And what about your brother?

Well, he's not one of them, is he?

And your niece? Her fiance?

Fuck. Why was he thinking of these people? They weren't his family. His family was standing in front of him, waiting to receive their spankings.

His family wasn't an Ex-Russian *Pakhan* and his daughter.

No.

Nope.

Not happening.

It was all these Thanksgiving invites. They had him all twisted up, not knowing which way was up and what was down.

That had to be it.

"Daddy? Are you okay?" Autumn asked.

"It's all these invites. I've never been invited to Thanksgiving or Christmas before."

"Oh." His Bunny's face filled with sympathy, which he didn't like. There was no reason to pity him. He was the greatest assassin the world had ever seen. He was an amazing Daddy and Papa. And a fantastic lover.

Oh, and did he mention rich and criminally good-looking?

Nope, no reason to pity him.

"You know what the problem is?" he said.

"Um, no, Papa," Brody said. "What's the problem?"

"I'm just too likable." He sighed. That was it. "I'm the person everyone wants at their party because I'm so damn charismatic. I make a party. Without me, all they'd have is a sad little gathering. Yep, that's it."

"That's right, Daddy," Autumn said loyally.

"Sure," Brody said. "But if you do accept any of the invites, then you have to promise not to harm anyone who annoys you."

He sighed heavily. "Back to this, huh?"

"Just think about it like this, Papa, if you harm anyone who annoys you at the, uh, parties, then are you going to be invited back?" Brody asked.

"Of course I am. I'm the life of any party.

"Have you ever been to something like this?" Autumn asked gently.

"What? A party? I've been to many."

"As yourself?" Brody asked.

He didn't like where they were going with this. He could feel himself closing up.

"Daddy, I know you won't really hurt anyone who annoys you," his Bunny said.

"Why do you say that?" he asked.

"Because you didn't harm that sales lady at the toy shop the other day and I could tell she really annoyed you."

"Ahh, that bitch," he drawled.

"Papa!" Brody chided. "Language."

"It's just the truth. She was a bitch."

"But you didn't hurt her," his Bunny said.

"Didn't I?" he asked.

Her eyes widened. "What did you do?"

"Hmm, well, I didn't harm her physically. But no one gets away with talking to my Bunny the way she did. I did a bit of research into her and guess what I found . . . not only was she cheating on her husband, but she was doing it with her boss. That bitch got kicked out by her hubby and fired when upper management was sent videos of her blowing her supervisor in the soft toy section of the store."

"Eww," Bunny said, screwing up her nose. "I hope I didn't touch anything that they did."

"You didn't. The things they did there were disgusting." He shuddered. "I had to sanitize myself after taking that video."

"She really was a bitch, Tutu," Brody added. "She deserved what she got."

"You knew?" she asked Brody.

His Pup shrugged. "Sure. I talked the Fox out of broadcasting their sexcapade on the shops PA system."

"I forgot about the children," the Fox said. "No need to scar them for life. So I had Brody anonymously send the video to upper management and they took care of it."

"You guys did that for me?" she whispered. "Because she was rude to me?"

"Nobody messes with my Bunny," he told her protectively.

"Yeah, no one," Brody added fiercely.

"Take off those tights and your tutu from around your ankles then come here," he commanded.

She managed to slip off her tights and tutu without falling over.

The Fox held out his arms. At the last moment, he reached down to cup his balls and cock.

He heard Brody let out a small laugh. But best to protect himself. She'd been known to take him down with one misplaced knee.

The Fox gathered her in against him, kissing the top of her head as she wrapped herself around him, her legs straddling his.

Brody slid his pants off his feet, then came and kneeled in front of him, cuddling in close to her back.

"I love our little family," Autumn told them. "I don't need anyone but the two of you."

He liked the sentiment. He never wanted his Bunny or Pup to be harmed and being around others meant there were factors that he couldn't account for.

She leaned back, looking up at him, then behind to Brody. "But Brody-bear needs to spend time with his family."

He did. As much as his Pup might complain about his sisters, the Fox knew he loved them.

"I really don't," Brody told them. "Only, if I don't turn up they'll probably call the cops. Or hound me endlessly until my dying days."

Poor, dramatic Pup.

"So we'll go to Pup's family for Thanksgiving," he said decisively. "They're family. It's only right."

He caught the relief on Brody's face. Had he been worried that he'd keep him away from them? All right, maybe that had occurred to him. He didn't always like the sound of these sisters. But he'd be there to keep them in their place. Wouldn't be hard. Six women, seven, if he counted Pup's mother. They'd be easy to tame and intimidate into behaving.

"But you have family too, Daddy," Autumn said softly.

What? Who?

Oh.

"You mean my sweet girl. Yes, we really should turn up there. Perhaps we can go there after we go to Pup's family? How long do we need to spend with your family, Pup? Like an hour?"

"Um, well, probably half the day."

He didn't like that idea.

"But we could likely arrive just before lunch, then eat and clean up. So maybe two, three hours max?"

"I don't like staying in one place that long with you both. But I have made your mother's house as safe as I can, so I suppose it should be all right. Two hours max, though."

"Wait, what?" Brody leaned back to look up at him in confusion. What was so hard to understand? "How did you make Momma's house safe?"

"Oh, I put in external cameras, and I have a warning alarm that goes off on my phone if anyone enters the property after a certain time of night. But I can change the time perimeters on that. She already had the security system that you put in. I just upgraded it a bit."

"You did that? For me?"

"Of course. She's your mother and you seem to care for her."

"I do. I love her. Thank you, Papa."

He reached out and cupped the side of his Pup's face. "You're welcome. I also put cameras up outside your sisters' houses."

"That's a lot of cameras," Brody joked. "You should have told me."

"I should have?" Hmm. That hadn't actually occurred to him. "You object?"

"No, I just. I would have thanked you properly."

"Interesting. With your mouth on my dick?"

"Daddy!" Autumn protested, but she was grinning. "I'm sure you can still do that, Brody-bear."

His Pup had grown red. He liked that he could still get embarrassed despite everything they'd done together.

"All right, Thanksgiving lunch at Brody's mother's. Dinner at my sweet girl's place. Sorted."

"Ah, does Sunny know that you're planning on us turning up?" Brody asked worriedly.

"Pfft. It's an open invitation. We can go for Christmas lunch too. As I said, they'd be grateful if I turned up. I'll even promise not to kill Duke."

"Magnanimous of you," Brody told him.

"I thought so."

"When I was talking about your family, Daddy, I wasn't meaning Sunny," Autumn told him.

He raised his eyebrows. "No?"

"We know Markovich asked you to his place for Thanksgiving and Christmas," Brody added.

"And just how would you know that?" he asked in a low, dangerous voice. "Have the two of you been snooping?"

"Just a little bit, Daddy."

"I maybe saw a text message on your phone," Brody explained.

Fuck it.

"I knew I should have blocked his number." He didn't know why he hadn't. He had no ties to the man.

"Aren't you going to at least think about going?" Autumn asked.

"Why should I? Blood doesn't make a family. I have no ties to him." Except he had worked with him a long time. There was a connection there. It just wasn't one he was certain that he wanted to cultivate.

"Are you sure, Papa? He seems to want to make one."

"Yes, he's quite desperate." The Fox sighed. "I feel sorry for him, really. I mean . . . I get it, who wouldn't want me as their family?" He pushed aside the thought of Markovich's brother, Pavel, who not only hadn't wanted to claim him but had been happy to see him beaten and left for dead.

"Exactly, Daddy. So shouldn't you try? Since he is. It's not . . . you are lucky to have some family who wants you."

He heard the note of pain in his Bunny's voice. Nope, that wouldn't do. He glanced over at Brody who was frowning.

"Bunny? Are you lonely here?"

"What?" she asked, staring up at him in surprise. "What do you mean? I have you and Brody-bear."

"But do you need more?" Brody asked. "Do you need friends?"

She tried to wriggle off the Fox's lap as she frowned.

"Bunny, stay still," he commanded.

"Let me off."

"No," he growled back at her. "Stay where you are."

She froze, staring up at him. He cupped her chin. "What is it?"

"I sound so pathetic. I've got no friends. No family."

Alarm filled him as she sniffled. He'd failed her. She obviously did need some friends.

"I shall get some for you."

"I'm not . . . you guys aren't going to go get me friends!" She stared up at him in horror.

"We didn't say that, Tutu." Brody moved around next to him on the floor.

"That's exactly what I said," the Fox pointed out.

His Bunny nodded and pushed her thumb into her mouth.

"Okay, but we're not going to do that," Brody said. "Maybe it's time to meet some of my friends, though. You'll like Ink's girlfriend, Betsy. She's very nice. And so is Sunny and the others."

"I suppose if we went to Markovich's at Thanksgiving then you could meet Emme and Dahlia." That would be a solution.

His Bunny slid the thumb out of her mouth, shaking her head. "No, Daddy. I don't want you to go for me. I want you to go for you."

That sounded like a load of garbage. He'd go for her.

Well, he'd think about it anyway.

He glanced down at his Pup and then at his Bunny. "It's time for your spankings."

Bunny squirmed at his look while his Pup grimaced. Yes, they should be worried. They'd been very naughty.

The Fox took them in for a moment. He didn't know what it said about him that he enjoyed having them kneeling by him as he sat. But he also didn't care.

"Why are you being punished, Pup?" he asked his boy first.

"For staying up too late."

"That's right. And for reading messages that you shouldn't on my phone."

"It was an accident."

He grunted. "And you, Bunny? Why are you about to get your butt spanked?"

"Um, 'cause I stayed up past my bedtime."

"Yes, and . . . ?"

She grimaced. "Because I went down the stairs on a toboggan."

"Yes, you could have been seriously hurt and that is completely unacceptable," he told her firmly. "Pup, you're up first. Stand and then lay yourself over my lap."

5

Fox, Brody, and Autumn

How did he keep finding himself in this position?

Brody stood slowly as Tutu slid back slightly. She better not try to run, the Fox wouldn't appreciate that. But she settled in, sending him a wink.

Ridiculously, he found himself grinning back. This wasn't exactly a smiling moment. This was an 'oh shit, I'm about to get my butt spanked by a man with a hand like a wooden paddle' sort of moment.

"Pup," the Fox said warningly. "Over you go."

"Yes, Papa." He lay over the Fox's lap. He always had a problem with being spanked like this.

Okay, with being spanked at all. Part of him liked it. And the other part of him found it weird that he liked it. That he wanted to go over the Fox's lap. It was a vulnerable position and it made him feel odd inside.

His younger side became more apparent when he was in this position.

"Daddy, you won't spank Brody-bear too hard, will you?" Tutu asked.

"Well, he was very naughty. Although not as naughty as you."

Uh-oh.

Before Brody could protest that he should have watched her more closely, the Fox landed a smack on his ass.

Holy. Crap.

That hurt.

Another landed. They kept coming in a steady wave that soon had Brody kicking his legs, small grunts coming from him as he wiggled around on the Fox's lap. He was certain he had to be getting heavy, but that didn't seem to affect the Fox. His hand landed over and over.

"Lie still, Pup. I don't want you to fall off my lap and hurt yourself."

Oh, the irony of that statement.

"Papa, no more!"

"I'm sorry, my Pup. There is definitely more to come. You know you were naughty, staying up so late."

"We was worried about you, Papa!"

"And I'm sorry about that. But you knew I was on my way home."

Damn it, yes, he had known.

A sob broke free as he lay on the Fox's lap and fully gave in to the spanking. The Fox moved his hand down to cover the tops of Brody's thighs. Ouch. He really wasn't going to sit well tomorrow.

Finally, he stopped, placing his hand on Brody's burning ass. "Next time, what are you going to do?"

"Call you, Papa."

"Good boy. Now, sit around on my lap so I can give you comfort. I know how to do that now. I dare say I'm an expert cuddler."

Brody shifted around so he could face the Fox, straddling his lap. He buried his face in the other man's chest as he held him.

"I could write a book on how to give aftercare," the Fox muttered.

And the thing was . . . he had become really good at aftercare. At cuddling. Giving comfort. Which Brody knew was something he struggled with. Or he had. He'd made himself learn how to do it for the two of them.

And what more could you ask for than that? Someone who was willing to do whatever was necessary in order to give you what you wanted. What you needed.

He was so fucking lucky to have the Fox. To have his Tutu.

The Fox continued to rub his back. "That's it, my Pup. Just let it all out. Good boy, you're such a good boy. I know you won't do this again. Or at least, you'll remember your sore bottom, won't you?"

"Yes, Papa."

He should probably feel embarrassed about sitting on the Fox's lap like this. Sometimes that was still a struggle for him. But today, it felt so right.

Finally, he reined himself in, sniffing back his tears.

"Do you need a tissue, Brody-bear?"

Turning his head, he saw Tutu kneeling, holding the tissues up. He nodded and reached for one. But the Fox lightly slapped his hand away.

"Let me."

Oh God.

He held himself still as the Fox wiped his face clean.

"Blow."

Jeez Lousie.

"Blow, Pup."

He wasn't Tutu who needed the Fox's help to clean herself up. But he also knew better than to protest. He didn't want to add to his spanking.

He blew his nose into the tissue.

"Good boy," the Fox crooned. "That wasn't so bad, was it?"

It really was. But he still didn't say anything.

"Are you feeling all right, my boy?" the Fox asked.

"Yes, Papa."

"Ready to go kneel while I take care of our girl?"

He nodded. "Yes."

"Good boy." The Fox placed a finger under his chin, tilting his face back so he could kiss him lightly. "Delicious."

A shiver ran up Brody's spine.

Brody climbed off the Fox's lap and kneeled down beside Autumn.

The Fox held out his hand to their girl. "Come here, Bunny."

OH, crap.

Why had she gone tobogganing down the stairs? It had seemed like such a good idea at the time.

Now . . . she was regretting it. Big time.

"Can we talk about this, Daddy?" she asked.

"Of course. Come lie over my lap for a nice chat."

That wasn't what she meant.

"But all the blood will rush to my head."

"Hmm, good point. All right, talk to me."

"Well, you see . . . um . . . I . . ." Shoot. Why hadn't she thought about what she was going to say? "I don't think I should be spanked for what I did, Daddy."

"No? You don't think staying up past your bedtime is naughty?" he asked.

"No, yes, I mean . . . that's not what you're most upset about though, Daddy!"

"Isn't it? What am I most upset about?"

"That I used the toboggan to ride down the stairs."

He leaned forward, his gaze intent on her. "And why would that upset me, baby girl?"

"Because you might worry that I would hurt myself. But I didn't! So you see . . . there's no reason to be upset and spank my poor little bottom."

She put her hands behind to cover her butt.

"No reason to be upset?" he asked in a low voice. "How much do you mean to me, baby girl?"

"Me and Brody are the most important things in the world to you. You'd kill for us, destroy for us, you'd even deal with pigeons for us. Because we are everything to you."

"That's right. And I don't want you to ever do anything that might endanger yourself. Either of you." He glanced over at Brody. "Understand me?"

"Yes, Daddy," she said.

"Yes, Papa," Brody agreed even though he hadn't done anything to put himself in harm's way.

"Now, do you honestly think you don't need a punishment for your behavior?"

She sighed. "No, I suppose I do."

He eyed her.

"I deserve a punishment, Daddy. I'm sorry for upsetting you."

"Thank you for apologizing. Come here." She took hold of his outstretched hand, then he drew her over his lap. "It's twenty spanks for you, baby girl. Ten for the toboggan and ten for staying up past your bedtime."

"Twenty, Daddy! That's too many."

"I am happy to make it twenty-five," he warned.

"But that's more than twenty, Daddy! You're supposed to do less not more!"

"Am I? Or I could just keep going up . . ."

"Twenty is good! Twenty is fine! I've always loved the number twenty," she blathered.

"Good. Enough talking. You both need to be put down for a nap."

Oh, bummer. She was really hoping he'd forget about that.

Yeah, who was she kidding? This was the Fox. He never forgot anything.

The first few smacks were always the worst in her opinion. They kind of took her breath away. And he didn't ease her into the spanking. He began as he meant to go on. Hard and heavy.

"Daddy, no! Please, no!" she cried out around halfway through.

"I'm sorry, baby. You're getting all twenty."

Of course she was. Because miracles didn't happen. Well, actually that wasn't true. They did. The proof was the man walloping her ass and the other one kneeling close by with his own red butt.

Yep, they were her miracles. But unfortunately, it seemed she wasn't going to be granted anymore. The last few spanks landed and she sobbed, all of her tension easing.

"That's it, baby girl. Good girl. It's all over. Just let it all out." The Fox rubbed his hand over her back as she cried.

"I'm s-sorry, D-daddy," she stuttered.

He helped her sit up, positioning her on his lap so she faced him. She pressed her face into his chest, where Brody's had been before and continued to cry as her poor bottom throbbed.

Gradually, she quieted, and the Fox drew her face back to look down at her. "I want you to be more careful with yourself because you are my everything."

"Y-yes, Daddy. You are my e-everything too."

His face tightened as he glanced at Brody then back to her. "I said I had retired, and I haven't done a good job of that, have I? Of taking care of the two of you."

"That's not true, Daddy!"

Brody shook his head. "We know you're doing something important and we support you."

"We told you to go do it," she added.

"But it's not as important as the two of you."

"I'm sorry, Daddy."

"Why are you sorry?" he asked.

"Because I was naughty while you were gone, and now you'll worry more about me when you're not here. I promise not to do anything naughty ever again."

The Fox grinned. "Don't make promises your butt can't pay the price for."

"Hey! Are you saying I'll still do naughty things?"

"Yep."

"Uh-huh," Brody added. "But that's part of the reason we love you."

"It is," the Fox told her quietly. "But I want you both to promise that if you need me, you'll call. Anytime."

"Promise," she said.

"I promise," Brody added.

"Come," he said, lifting her off his lap and standing. She walked over and grabbed Freddy Fox.

He held his hands out for each of them. "Time for a nap."

They each took a hand and let him lead them toward the nursery.

"Papa, I don't really need to nap, right?" Brody asked.

He rarely put his Pup down for a nap. "Yes, you do. You're tired and you need some rest. You can sleep in Tutu's bed and she'll go down in her crib."

"Can't I go sleep in our bed?" he asked. "This is a nursery."

"I'm starting to think you might need another spanking," he said warningly.

"Sorry, Papa. I'm good."

Yeah, that's what he thought. "Do either of you need to go potty?"

They both shook their heads. So he led his baby girl over to the changing table. He lifted her up onto it. She winced as her bottom rested against the pad on the top of the table.

"Ouch, Daddy."

"Poor baby. Stay there while I get your onesie and training panties." He grabbed the thick panties out, then slid them under her bottom and between her legs before doing them up at the sides. By now, she was sucking on her thumb and looked like she was half-asleep.

After stripping off her other top, he quickly got her dressed in a onesie that had pictures of cute bunnies all over it. Picking her up, he carried her to her crib and laid her down. She hugged Freddy Fox tight.

"Butt-butt sore," she muttered, drifting further into Little headspace.

"That's because you were naughty."

"Naughty Daddy."

"I don't think so."

"Uh-huh."

"How am I naughty?" he asked curiously.

She shrugged. "Spanked my butt-butt." She gave him a look like it was obvious.

Right. Sometimes he forgot that in Little headspace her

arguments weren't always logical. Actually, they often weren't logical.

Reaching over into a nightstand drawer, he drew out the pacifier with a fox on it. She took it eagerly, her eyes starting to drift shut. He'd known she needed a nap.

When he heard her breathing slow, he turned to his Pup and took him in. Fuck, he was gorgeous. The urge to play with the other man came over him.

No. No playing. No edging. Nap.

Sometimes, it was hard to be in charge.

Nah, who was he kidding? He loved being the one in control. He was born for this.

"I don't need a nap, Papa."

He took time to study his Pup. There were dark smudges under his eyes and a hint of strain around his mouth. He'd worked longer hours than the Fox would like lately. However, the Fox knew his work was important to him, so he'd allowed it. But that on top of last night was showing on his face.

The Fox walked over to him. He could order him into bed. Give him a smack on the bottom to get him moving.

But he went for option three. He drew the other man into his chest, wrapping his arms around him. His Pup was stiff for a long moment. Did he not want a hug?

Nah, of course he did. People would kill for a hug this good.

Brody gradually relaxed against him. He rubbed his hand up and down the smaller man's back.

"I wasn't expecting this."

Ahh. So that's why he was so tense? Because he'd thought he'd go for one of the other options? The old Fox likely would have. But he was a changed man.

Ha-ha not really. But when it came to them, he'd learned that he liked putting them first. Their needs and wants. They were what was important to him.

So he held his Pup until he slumped against him.

"You're tired, my boy."

"I'll be all right until bedtime. I'm a big boy."

"Not right now. At the moment, you're my baby boy. And you're going to be good for Papa and climb into bed to have a nap. When you wake up, we'll spend the rest of the day playing and watching movies. Okay?"

"Okay, Papa. I've got some Legos to build. Tutu wants a princess tower for her dolls."

"We can do that. We'll make the best princess tower that the world has ever seen. Now, you sit on the bed while I get your *Spiderman* pajamas." He walked over and grabbed them from the wardrobe.

Brody stood when he got close, reaching for them. "I can do it, Papa."

"No. You can't. Now, I believe I told you to sit."

Pup grimaced. "But it hurts."

"That's the point of a spanking," he replied mildly. "Sit."

Brody sat with a sigh that let the Fox know he was very put out.

Tough.

The Fox stripped off his Pup's T-shirt before grabbing his pajamas. Crouching, he put the pajama bottoms over his feet, then tugged them up over his knees. Then he moved back slightly to give the other man some room. "Stand up, Pup."

Brody stood, and his dick was right in the Fox's face. Well, he was never one to turn down an opportunity like that. Opening his mouth, he took the Pup's dick inside his mouth in one long movement.

Brody let out a low moan. "Sir."

He slid his mouth back along his shaft, then licked the head before drawing back and returning to his previous task.

A whimper escaped his Pup as he drew the pajama bottoms up, then stood.

"Sir, please."

"Uh-uh. You don't get to come. But if you're a good boy and have your nap, then I might wake you up with my mouth on your cock."

"It's a deal."

Yeah, he thought he would say that.

6

Fox, Autumn, and Brody

IT WAS THANKSGIVING.

The Fox had never celebrated Thanksgiving before. He had never really understood it. What had there been to be thankful for?

Well, he guessed he should be thankful to be so good at his chosen career. His ability to kill and not get caught was legendary.

But he was always thankful for that.

"Here we go," Brody muttered.

They were all standing at the bottom of the footpath, looking at the small house. It was older but looked after well. Still, the Fox wasn't sure he approved of this neighborhood. Perhaps Brody could talk his mother into a house in a better area.

"Are you sure you want to do this?" his Pup asked. "Once you go in, there's no getting out. You're part of them, and they'll never let you go."

His Bunny glanced around him to stare at Brody. "They're not a cult, Brody-bear."

"Are you so sure?" Brody asked. "Because I'm not."

He didn't like how stressed his Pup was. "If you don't want to go, then we won't. We'll walk away and never return."

His Pup gaped up at him. "We can't do that."

Huh? He was confused. Didn't he just tell them to walk away?

"You're stressed, and I don't like it," he stated.

"Yeah, but that doesn't mean I want to leave. They're family. Plus, they'll have seen us by now. They'll chase us down like a screaming pack of hyenas and rip the flesh from our bones."

He stiffened. What the fuck?

"Uh, Brody-bear?" Autumn said.

"Yeah?"

"You might want to tone it down a bit before we lose Daddy and get the Fox."

What did that mean? He was always the Fox.

Brody peered up at him, his eyes widening at whatever he saw. "But this will be fun. It will be great. They're lovely people. You'll adore them." He fiddled nervously with his glasses.

"I am confused."

"Brody's just worried about us making a good impression on his family," Bunny explained, running her hand up and down his arm soothingly. "He's nervous."

"Why would he be nervous about that?" he asked. "Of course we'll make a good impression. Are you saying that Bunny will do something to embarrass you?"

"What? No! Of course not!" Brody said, looking horrified.

"Well, I know you aren't thinking that about me."

"I'm not . . . I'm not worried about you guys embarrassing me. It's the opposite."

"About you embarrassing us?" the Fox asked. "You could never do that, my Pup."

"No. It's them . . . you have no idea what they're like."

"Then we walk," he stated.

"But I can't walk." Brody sighed. "It's hard to explain."

"Families are complicated," Autumn agreed.

Hmm, yes, he was beginning to understand that.

"Then let's simplify things. If they are mean to either of you, we leave. Then I'll come back and rip the flesh from their bones."

"Fox, we discussed this," his Pup told him. "What did you agree to?"

He sighed. This was ridiculous.

"Daddy," Autumn said.

"Fine. I agreed I wouldn't harm any member of your family, even if they were mean or annoyed me." However, that meant physical harm. Ensuring their lives were miserable wasn't part of the agreement.

Both of his babies were staring up at him.

"I'll be good," he promised.

Yeah, right.

Taking both of their hands in his, he led them toward the door.

Brody was nearly peeing himself with nerves.

His sisters were going to embarrass him. He just knew it. It was inevitable. They seemed to think it was their main purpose in life.

That wasn't what was stressing him out, though. Nope, mostly he was concerned about how the Fox would react.

The Fox leaned in to whisper in his ear. "Calm down, or I will pick you up and carry you out of here."

Right. He didn't want that.

Reaching out, he opened the door. His palms slipped. He was sweating, despite how cold it was out here.

When the door finally opened, he let out a low groan. Yep, it was as bad as he'd thought. Because standing there in the foyer were all six of his sisters. And they were all wearing T-shirts with photos of him on the front.

Naked photos of him.

And not all of them were from when he was a kid.

His oldest sister, Jodie, had a photo of him when he got drunk at his twenty-first birthday party and they'd stripped him to put him to bed.

"You guys are a bunch of jerks."

He heard a stifled giggle and glanced over at Tutu. But she had her head turned away.

"Aww, Boo-boo, don't you like our T-shirts?" Jodie asked. Her long hair was bleached almost white and cut into a bob.

"You can't tell me that Ma has seen those," he said.

"Course not," Lissy said, dimples appearing as she grinned. They all drew their cardigans over the images. They were all ugly Christmas sweaters.

He groaned. "I am not taking a family photo wearing one of those."

"You will," Anna sang. Her dark hair was up in pigtails today and she looked so young.

They were all awful. And he had no idea what he was doing here. Finally, he realized how hard the Fox was holding his hand and he glanced up at him.

"It's just in good fun," he whispered to him.

"You're upset."

"I'm fine. Promise."

"What is going on out here? Why are you all in the foyer? Come in. Come in."

Brody instantly relaxed at his Momma's voice. She stepped in, staring at his sisters suspiciously. They all stared back innocently.

"Uh-huh," she muttered. Then she turned toward them. Brody braced himself. This was his Momma. He loved his sisters. But it was his Momma who held his heart. Who had the power to destroy him if she didn't accept his unusual relationship. He'd warned them all. But it was a different thing to meet the people he lived with.

However, no matter what any of them thought, he was never giving up his Tutu or his Sir.

"My boy," she said, stepping forward, her whole body softening. She wrapped him up in a hug.

She moved back, holding his arms. "Look at you. Are you getting thinner? Have you been eating?"

"You know he only eats pizza and burgers, Momma," Nina said.

He stuck his tongue out at her over his mother's shoulder.

"You need to eat better. We'll get some veggies into you."

"He's eating well," the Fox said smoothly. "I'm making sure of that."

His mother turned to the Fox and Brody's breath caught in his lungs. Oh shit.

"Is that so?" she murmured. "You must be Raev?"

Brody bit his lip nervously. The Fox had given them one of his personas to use with Brody's family and any friends who didn't know his identity.

"Yes, hello," the Fox said smoothly. "Raev Foxhill, but please feel free to call me Fox." He held out his hand and his mother shook it.

Okay. So far so good.

"Call me Bella." She still eyed him suspiciously. "You're taking care of my son?"

"Always. His wellbeing and happiness are very important to me."

Brody sucked in a breath. Wow. How did the Fox know just what to say?

His mother nodded. "Good." She wasn't won over yet, but he knew that the Fox had to have earned some brownie points.

Then she moved her gaze to Autumn who was half-hiding behind the Fox, staring out at them all nervously. He knew his momma wouldn't fail to fall in love with his Tutu.

"And you must be Autumn."

"It's a pleasure to meet you, ma'am," Tutu whispered.

"Call me Bella." She reached out and took Autumn's hand in hers. "Come. Let's find you something to eat. You look hungry."

Okay, he hadn't thought she'd fall that quickly for Autumn. Tutu gave him a startled look, but he just smiled back at her. Autumn could use a family and he was happy to share his. Especially if it got his sisters off his back. He couldn't believe those T-shirts.

They were the worst.

"Come, take off your jackets," his mother said. "Come in and make yourselves at home."

"Hey, aren't you going to introduce us?" Jodie complained.

He sighed as they all walked into the small living area. Everyone found somewhere to perch, leaving him standing with the Fox while his mother tugged Autumn toward the kitchen, asking her what her favorite food was.

"I was hoping to forget you all exist," he muttered.

"Aww, Boo-boo, didn't you like our gift?" Nina said.

"We were just trying to be welcoming," Lissy added.

"It wasn't nice," the Fox suddenly stated. "You embarrassed him. Don't do that again."

They all gaped at the Fox, including him.

Oh. Shit.

Even his mother and Autumn turned back from the doorway. Tutu gave him an alarmed look.

Yep. He got that.

"Ah, Fox," he muttered, moving closer to the man.

"Yeah? And who is going to stop us?" Sam asked, fiddling with her glasses. She was usually the quietest, but that didn't mean she was to be underestimated. Nope. She was sneakier than the rest of them put together. Those T-shirts had been her idea.

The Fox folded his arms over his chest. "I am."

Brody braced himself for the explosion.

"Whoa, that was hot," Lissy whispered.

Wait. What?

He looked over at the doorway, but luckily his mother and Tutu were gone.

Why weren't they all screaming? Why weren't they trying to cut the Fox off at the knees?

"Yeah, you can say that again," Jodie said.

"Totally sexy," Nina added. "And I never thought I'd say that about anyone Boo-boo brought home."

"We always figured no one would be worthy of our baby brother," Lola said. She walked over to the Fox, wrapping her arm around his. "But you . . . we like you."

They all nodded in agreement.

"What is happening?" he asked in bewilderment. "What's wrong with you all? Oh my God! It finally happened. Zombies ate your brains."

"Boo-boo, you're always so dramatic," Jodie said.

"If zombies ate our brains, wouldn't we be zombies?" Nina asked.

Anna was tugging the Fox over to a chair. And for some

reason, he was allowing it. What was he doing? Why was he letting his sister pull him around?

What would you rather? That he protested? You've been the one begging him not to do anything to scare your sisters.

Although, he'd thought that the Fox's words would have pissed them off. Instead, they were acting like he was royalty. Lissy sat on his other side while the others crowded around while he stood there, feeling completely off kilter. They were all pestering the Fox with questions.

"Pod people," he said.

They all went silent, staring up at him.

Nina sighed loudly. "Brody, we haven't been taken over by pod people."

"Are you sure?" he asked.

The Fox stood.

"Where are you going?" Anna asked, staring up at him.

"My Pup needs me and I've lost track of my girl."

Brody gulped. Were they going to say something about him calling Brody his pup?

"Pup?" Amusement filled Jodie's eyes.

"Well, he does have cute puppy dog eyes," Lissy said.

Brody groaned. "Just stop."

"Yeah, but he's not like a Rottweiler pup," Nina said, flicking her long dark hair over her shoulder.

"No, more like a chihuahua," Jodie said.

"No way," Lissy protested. "Chihuahuas can be vicious. I think he's one of those teddy bear dogs. Cute and cuddly."

He groaned. They were seriously going to be the death of him.

The Fox stepped up. "There's nothing wrong with cute and cuddly."

"Who knew that sweet little Boo-boo, who spent most of his

time playing alone in his bedroom, would have such a hot boyfriend," Jodie mused.

"And girlfriend," Nina added. "Maybe we should go ask her if he's treating her right."

Brody stepped back, pointing at them all. "No. Nope. Do not start. Come on, Fox. Let's find Tutu."

"Pup," the Fox said warningly as he drew him out of the room.

"Let's get Tutu. We need to leave."

Suddenly, he found himself turned and pressed against the wall. The Fox crowded in on him, his hands either side of his head.

"What are you doing? Someone might see us," he asked nervously.

The Fox shoved his leg between Brody's, placing his thigh against his firm dick. He whimpered.

"Fox."

"What do you call me?"

"Sir. They're going to walk in here."

"So?" the Fox asked. He cupped the side of his face. "I don't care what they do, what they think, or say. All I care about is you and our girl and the way they affect you. You're upset."

He sighed. "You're not upset by anything they said?"

"No. Like I said, all that concerns me is the two of you. So do you want to leave?"

Did he? "No."

"You tell me if that changes, I'll grab you both and we're gone."

Brody gave him a small smile. "Thank you, Sir."

"You're welcome, my Pup." He kissed him. It was so hot that it made his legs go weak and he found himself leaning on the Fox's thigh between his. Not that the Fox seemed to care.

Please, dick. Don't get hard. Please.

But as usual, that asshole didn't listen to a word he said. By the time the Fox drew back, his cock was throbbing and pressing hard against his jeans.

A throat clearing had him drawing back and looking down the passage to see his sisters all crowding around, staring at them.

He braced himself for the onslaught.

Nightmare.

Please don't let his sisters see how hard he was.

"Wow, I don't know how I feel about that," Lissy said.

"I feel a lot of mixed emotions," Jodie added.

"Do you have a brother, Fox?" Nina asked, peering up at the Fox.

"Or five or six," Jodie added.

"Hey, some of us have boyfriends," Lola said, chewing her gum loudly. Her blonde hair had pink streaks that he personally loved.

"What you have is an asshole who treats you as a convenient lay," Nina told her.

"What?" Brody asked. "He isn't treating you right? Who? I want his name."

"Aww, Boo-boo is getting all protective," Anna said. "That's so sweet."

He dropped it for now, but he'd get that name later.

"What are you all doing in here?" Brody's mother came into the hallway, Autumn walking behind her with her eyes wide. "You're all behaving very strangely. Nina, Anna, and Jodie, get into the kitchen to help me. Lissy, get our guests a drink."

"They're not guests, though, Momma," Lissy pointed out. "They're family. Can't they get their own drinks?"

"You go do as you were told, girl," his mother snapped back. "You're not too old for me to take you over my knee."

"A woman after my own heart," the Fox whispered in his ear.

Dear Lord, save him.

He knew this had been a bad idea.

His Momma shooed them all off, then turned to him. "What did they do?"

"What?" he asked.

She flicked him around the head, and he tightened his hold on the Fox, not wanting him to retaliate. "This is my Momma."

"Why are you telling him that?" his mother asked. "He knows I'm your momma."

Yes, but he wanted to remind the Fox that she was off-limits, no matter what she did to him.

But to his shock, the Fox remained relaxed.

"Well?" she demanded.

Brody sighed, knowing she wouldn't let it go. "They made T-shirts and printed photos of me naked on them."

His mother's lips twitched. But she managed to get herself under control. Yes, everyone thought it was hilarious.

Ha-ha.

"No dessert for them," his mother declared.

"No, don't do that, Momma. You know that will make them worse."

"No. Then there is more for the little one here." She lightly patted Autumn's back. Poor Tutu. She looked like she was in shock. "She needs it. Brats, the lot of them."

She walked away, muttering.

The Fox immediately stepped back and reached his hand for Autumn's, taking hold and drawing her close.

"Are you all right, Tutu? Is it too much?" Brody asked her.

"It . . . no. Of course not."

"Baby girl, look at me." The Fox waited for her to raise her gaze to his. "Do not lie."

She flinched slightly, giving Brody an apologetic look. "It's a lot."

"We can leave—" he started to say.

"But it also isn't," she said in a confused voice. "She told me to call her Momma."

"What?" Brody asked, shocked.

"Yeah . . . I . . . what just happened?"

Brody wrapped his arms around behind her, kissing her cheek. "She accepted you. You're family."

"I . . . I am?"

"Uh-huh, and once my momma accepts you, then you're in for life." He didn't know how it had happened so quickly. Jodie, Nina, and Sam had all been married, and their husbands had never been invited to call her momma. And they were all divorced now.

"But why?" she asked, sounding so bewildered that it broke his heart.

"Because she saw what a beautiful person you are," he told her. "Welcome to the family, Tutu."

"Ohh." She buried her face in the Fox's chest.

"So when she lets you call her momma you're accepted?" the Fox asked.

"Uh, yeah, but don't be upset," he said hastily. "She never accepted any of my sisters' husbands or boyfriends."

"Yes, but they were all fools."

It shouldn't surprise him that the Fox had researched his sisters and their partners.

"And challenge accepted."

Oh heck.

7

Fox, Brody, and Autumn

Autumn sat between the Fox and Brody at the large dining table. They'd managed to keep her between them since she left the kitchen with Brody's mother, who was both the sweetest and scariest woman that she'd ever met.

How she'd managed to raise seven kids on her own, Autumn had no idea. And most of them were outspoken and crazy. The only exceptions seemed to be Brody and Sam.

Autumn pushed the food around on her plate. That trick with the naked photos of Brody on their T-shirts had been genius and a little mean.

She wished she was as confident as these women. While their teasing could get out of hand, it was also clear how much they loved each other. And Brody.

And they seemed to have taken an interest in the Fox.

"So, Fox, you work in security?" Anna asked.

"Yes," he replied.

"That's how you met Boo-boo?" Nina asked.

"It is. Mrs McClain, this food is delicious," the Fox said smoothly.

"Why, thank you, Mr. Foxhill."

"Please, I insist you call me Fox."

Autumn turned to gape at him, aware of Brody doing the same thing from her other side.

Who was this? And what happened to the Fox who had no social grace or manners?

"What?" he whispered in her ear. "I read a book on what to do the first time you meet your in-laws. Wasn't so hard to learn. You think a man who knows a hundred and eighteen ways to kill a person can't figure out how to get on someone's good side?"

"I think you've never tried to get on someone's good side."

"Exactly," he grinned. "So how do you know I wouldn't be any good at it? Far as I can tell I'm smashing it. I knew I would. There's nothing I can't do."

Dear Lord.

Brody reached for her hand under the table, squeezing it. She got it.

Who was this version of the Fox?

Then it hit her. The Fox was in disguise, like he always was when he left the house. He often put on a persona around other people, but never when he was with just the two of them. Right now, he was a mix of both. Outwardly, he was Raev Foxhill, a security specialist and investor. Inside, he was still their Fox. He just had a thin veneer of civility. Hopefully, no one would see that most of this was a pretense.

"Eat, baby girl," he whispered in her ear as Brody's sisters started to compete about who could tell the most embarrassing Brody story. Yikes, they had some fascinating ones.

"I'm not hungry," she said back quietly.

"I'm sorry, baby," he said in a voice that told her he wasn't really sorry. "But that wasn't a request."

A shiver raced up her spine at his voice.

Jeepers.

And there he was.

"So, Autumn, tell us, did you enjoy the present we got you last year?" Anna asked, brushing back her unruly curls.

Oh, crap.

Her face grew red. She glanced around, but saw that Brody's mom must have left the room.

"Oh…um…I…"

"Guessing you don't really need it with two men, though," Sam added. "How does that work?"

Yep, her face was so hot she felt like she was about to expire. Had they really asked her that? And in front of their brother?

"You guys are the worst," Brody groaned.

"What?" Lola asked. "It was a legit question. Is it like one after the other or both together?"

Brody's hand landed over her mouth, making her frown. What did he think she was going to say?

"You do not need to answer that," Brody told her.

She drew his hand from her mouth.

"Hey, don't you boss her around, Boo-boo," Nina said.

"Yeah, don't you take any shit from him or either of them, girl," Anna said.

"We got your back," Jodie added. "We know just how to take care of baby brother if he needs some manners."

"He doesn't," she said fiercely, surprising herself. But she wouldn't have them malign Brody. "He's perfect the way he is. And he'd never bully or hurt me or anything like that. He saved me. I love him."

There was silence.

"And in answer to your other question, it works just fine. Mighty, mighty fine."

They all stared at each other, then smiled at her widely. What was happening?

"Welcome to the family, sis," Jodie told her.

Had it been some sort of test?

"Yeah, anyone who loves this idiot that much is good by us," Anna said, rubbing Brody's head affectionately.

"I'd appreciate it if you didn't call him an idiot," the Fox said in a stern voice.

It was clear they were all slightly confused by the Fox, but they ignored him, continuing with the who could embarrass Brody more stories.

"They have terrible survival instincts," she whispered to Brody.

He stared at them, aghast. "I know. They don't even know who is eating dinner with them."

"But we do." She grasped his hand, then turned to the Fox, taking his hand in hers. "And I'm so thankful for the two of you."

They left about an hour later. She hadn't eaten much. Her tummy had been filled with nerves, even though his family had been really welcoming. They'd tried to make her and Fox join them for their ugly sweater photo. Thankfully, they hadn't had any spare sweaters.

Poor Brody-bear. They'd chosen an awful sweater for him.

Brody's mother followed them out.

"Momma, thank you for lunch," Brody said, kissing her cheek. His hands were full of containers of leftover food. There was so much food that she didn't know what they were going to do with it all. But none of his sisters had blinked at the amount Brody gathered up, which made her think it was a regular occurrence for him.

His sisters had all given her hugs goodbye. They'd even

dared to hug the Fox. Nobody else had likely seen the way he'd stiffened. Luckily, Raev Foxhill didn't seem to object to a bunch of women hugging him.

Well, not out loud anyway.

"Anytime. You'll come back soon." It was a demand rather than a question.

"Yes, Momma."

She turned to Autumn and took her gently into her arms. "You barely ate anything."

"I'm sorry." She hoped she didn't insult the other woman. "Nerves."

"From dealing with that lot. The next time you come back, we'll have dinner without them. I love them, but they're a lot."

Whew. She was glad the other woman understood. She sent her a warm smile. "Thank you for today."

Brody's mother brushed off her thanks, but she could tell she was pleased. Then she turned to the Fox. She glanced down at his hands, where he wasn't holding any food containers. Brody's mom was probably wondering why he wasn't offering to carry anything and instead was letting Brody take it all.

"Here, let me help, Brody," she offered, holding out her arms.

The Fox grunted and Brody shook his head. "I got it. I'm used to carrying food out of here."

Then Brody's mom surprised her by nodding. "You protect them both."

"Always," the Fox said.

"Good. My boy deserves people who love him. He's special."

"Aww, Ma, you have to say that," Brody said. "But luckily, I like hearing it."

The Fox placed his hand on the small of her back and she turned to walk down to the car.

"Sorry we can't stay," Brody said. "I'll call you tomorrow. Love you."

"Love you, my boy."

The Fox opened the backdoor and she climbed into her car seat, hoping that Brody's mom couldn't see that she sat in a booster seat. The Fox did up her belt, then helped Brody load the containers into the trunk.

Brody sat in the front seat, letting out a sigh. "That was a lot. I'm so sorry."

"Why are you sorry?" she asked. "Your family is crazy . . . but it's also obvious how much love they have for each other."

Still, she would be happy to go home. She drew Freddy Fox out from where she'd had him in her bra. She knew it was a risk that he would fall out, but she couldn't have gone into a new situation like that one without him. Lying back, she put her thumb in her mouth.

The Fox turned to look at her. The car was still idle. He'd gone out about ten minutes before they left to check the vehicle over. He was paranoid about car bombs.

Probably because he'd used them himself in the past.

"Tired, baby girl?"

It was still pretty early but she nodded.

"I wonder if I should drop you both off home then." He reached down for her blankie, pulling it over her lap. The blanket had a Fox's face on it, complete with ears that stuck out.

"Where are you going?" Brody asked.

"Thought I'd go see some people. They've been begging. Perhaps it's time to see them."

"Who, Sunny and Duke?" Brody asked. "Do they know you're coming?"

"Not Sunny and Duke. Markovich."

She gaped at the Fox, taking her thumb from her mouth.

"But since you're tired, baby girl, I'll take you both home first."

"No way," she croaked.

"We're coming," Brody added.

He glanced at them both, his eyebrows raised. "Who is in charge?"

"You are, Daddy. But we wanna go and support you."

He frowned. "I don't know. It might not be safe."

"You'll be with us," Brody pointed out. "How could we be safer? And wouldn't Markovich's house be safer than here?"

The Fox grunted. But she knew they almost had him.

"Please, Daddy. Please." She gave him her best puppy dog eyes.

He pointed at her. "I'm going to spank you later for trying to manipulate me and top from the bottom. But yes, you can both come."

8

Markovich and Dahlia

Dahlia opened the oven door and stared at the turkey. Surely it was cooked by now. She'd followed the instructions exactly.

Okay, not exactly.

But she figured it would be okay.

Today had to be perfect. She wanted to give Dimitri a Thanksgiving to remember. Something that would take his mind off everything. Even though he was doing a lot better than he had been right after his brother and wife were killed, sometimes he still went to dark places.

And it didn't help that the Fox kept ignoring his invites to connect.

If she ever saw that bastard . . . she'd do . . . well, she'd give him . . . okay, she likely wouldn't do much of anything because she'd be too intimidated. She still didn't understand how he'd found not one but two people who were brave enough to be with him.

Boggled her mind.

Markovich was in his office, working. She sighed. She hoped he wasn't planning on working all the way through Christmas. Yesterday, she'd set up all the Christmas decorations. She'd hoped he would notice, but he hadn't said anything. Not that she was blaming him or anything . . . okay, it was a bit odd. Especially as she'd put some up really high and she'd felt sure he would freak out over the fact that she'd gotten up a ladder to install them.

Still, nothing.

Sighing, she tried to find some oven mitts so she could safely take out the turkey. She'd never cooked one of these before. But she needed to take it out so she could put the sweet potato casserole in.

Since Maria had left for a week to spend time with her family, she didn't have anyone to help her. And Reyes and Emme were due in a couple of hours.

Gray had gone with Maeve to spend Thanksgiving and Christmas with her friends, which had made Dahlia feel even lonelier.

She still couldn't believe that Markovich's wife had been alive all that time. That she and Pavel had really been in charge of the whole trafficking ring. That Galina had been working in the background this entire time.

That she hadn't cared about Dimitri at all. Who wouldn't fight to stay with Dimitri?

Selfish bitch.

Ruthless prick.

They'd both cared more about power and money than they had about family. Not that she would have wanted Galina to step back into Dimitri's life. Since that meant Dahlia wouldn't have him.

And she needed him more than she needed to breathe.

Finally, she gave up on the oven mitts and just grabbed two towels. Opening the door, she coughed as a wave of heat hit her. She'd put the temperature up extra high to make up time. But sheesh, that was hot enough to singe her eyebrows.

Grabbing the base of the tray, she heaved. But the towels slipped and the turkey toppled sideways, slipping off the pan and falling onto the oven door. She let out a scream as it slid across the door, then onto the floor. She leaped for it, but unfortunately, she forgot that the oven door was open. Her shin hit the edge and she nearly toppled forward onto the door. At the last moment, she managed to shove herself backward, falling onto her butt on the floor.

Her butt protested the harsh treatment. And she burst into tears.

"Dahlia? L'venok, where are you?" Dimitri came running into the room. Horror filled his face as he took in the open oven, the turkey on the floor, and her sitting there on her ass, with tears streaming down her face.

"Baby! Baby girl, what happened? Are you burned? Where are you hurt?" He rushed in and landed beside her on his knees, running his hands over her. "Baby, talk to me. Where are you hurt?" His voice was growing frantic.

"I'm o-okay," she sobbed, trying to get herself under control.

"I'll get a car pulled around and we'll take you to the emergency room."

"No! No, I don't need to go to the hospital."

"Baby, you've burned yourself!"

"I didn't."

He gave her a skeptical look.

"Really," she insisted. "I was getting the turkey out, but I couldn't find the oven mitts, so I used a couple of towels to protect my hands. Only, they slipped when I was pulling the turkey out of the oven, and it . . . it went flying." She covered her face with her hands.

"Baby, how did you end up on the floor?"

"I tripped," she wailed. "I went to get the turkey as it flew around like it had wings. Stupid turkey."

"Dahlia, focus. You tripped?"

"I forgot the oven door was open and my legs hit it."

"Oh baby, are they bruised?" He gently prodded at her shins and she hissed.

"Daddy, don't! Hurts."

"Shit. You could have fallen onto the oven door."

"I nearly did. I managed to throw my weight back so I didn't fall on it."

She noticed how still he'd grown.

"But I'm okay," she said hastily. "Better than the turkey is, anyway. Dumb turkey. Why'd it have to go flying like that? Doesn't it know it no longer has wings?" Her Little was pushing forward. Mainly because she was upset and wanted some comfort. Her shins hurt. Her butt hurt. And her pride hurt.

Not only that, but her Thanksgiving dinner was ruined, and all she had were some meals that Maria had frozen before she left. Which would likely taste better than anything she could make, anyway.

"Baby girl, you could have really hurt yourself," he scolded. "You should have called me instead of trying to pull that turkey out yourself." He closed the oven before holding out his hands to her. She let him pull her up, then he picked her up and set her on the counter.

"You were busy," she muttered, staring down at her lap.

Darn it, her shins were really throbbing now.

This day sucked monkey balls.

"Look at me." He placed a finger under her chin, tilting her head back. "I am never too busy for you."

"I know, Daddy." Deep down she did. But it just seemed that lately he had a lot going on. Or maybe he acted like he did in order to try and forget about other stuff in his life.

"You came so close to burning yourself," he said, sounding horrified. "From now on, I don't want you touching the oven."

She gaped at him. "But, Daddy—"

"No, you're forbidden from touching it. Do not test me on this."

She gulped. She'd noticed that he had grown more protective since everything had happened. Not that she minded, exactly. But there might come a point where enough was enough.

Just have some patience with him.

"I need to use the oven."

"Why? Maria does most of the cooking. If she's not here, then you'll ask for help. But no touching the oven or it's your butt that will burn."

She groaned. "That was terrible, Daddy."

"What was?" He frowned, then obviously realized what he'd said. "Oh yeah. That was good."

It hadn't been good.

"But, Daddy, how will I cook the sweet potato casserole? And I have to make the gravy. Oh man, I need to get the turkey off the freaking floor!"

How had she forgotten about the turkey?

She tried to wriggle down.

"Stay still," he told her.

"But Daddy, I gots to get the turkey."

"No," he said firmly. "You need to sit there and let me take care of you. The turkey can wait."

"I've totally ruined Thanksgiving dinner!" she cried. "There's only going to be floor turkey and uncooked potato casserole. I'm the worst girlfriend ever!"

She'd be lying if she said it hadn't played on her mind a bit . . . the fact that she was living with Dimitri while his wife had still been alive. It wasn't like either of them had known . . . but if he had, would he have chosen her?

"Dahlia? What's wrong?" he asked.

"Nothing." She smiled at him brightly. "I'm good as gold. Hunky-dory. Totally A-Okay. Couldn't get more okay than me."

"Right." He gave her a skeptical look.

She might have gone overboard while trying to convince him she was all right. Hopefully, he didn't press her further.

Someone must have heard her prayers because he wrapped his hands around her hips. "I need to check your shins. Let's get those tights off." He lifted her down off the counter, holding onto her until he made sure that she was steady before reaching for the waistband of her tights. Then he slid them down her legs, crouching to pull them off her feet. She held onto his shoulders as he took them off.

"Oh, L'venok, these look sore," he told her, running his hand lightly over her legs. Then he stood and lifted her up onto the counter again. "I'm going to get you some ice."

"They're okay," she told him. "I'm fine. I really should get the casserole into the oven."

He shot her a look before lifting her legs onto the counter and placing some ice over them. "Just sit there, and I'll put the casserole in the oven. And deal with the turkey." He popped the casserole in first before picking up the turkey and setting it on the counter.

"Do you think we can wash it off? I mean, with water only. Not with dish soap or anything. That would be kind of gross. No one likes the taste of dish soap. Yuck. I accidentally had some once and I spent the whole day blowing bubbles. Not really, but you get the idea—"

"Baby, chill," Dimitri told her in a low voice.

Chill? Did she know how to chill?

"Deep breath in. Now, let it out slowly. That's it. In. Out. Good girl."

She found herself calming down. He was always able to do that for her.

Her rock.

Would he have chosen her?

Stop worrying about this. It doesn't matter. He's yours now. You don't have to stress.

"You okay, baby girl?"

"Yeah, Daddy. I'm good." She managed a smile for him. It didn't matter. She had him, and she wasn't going to waste any more time thinking about her.

At least, that's what she told herself.

"All right, let's have a look at this turkey." He turned to the turkey, frowning down at it before he moved to a drawer, rummaging through it until he found a long metal skewer. He pushed it into the bird.

"It should be done," she said. "It's been in there for ages."

"Baby, it's frozen in the middle."

"What? Nooo." This was it. Now Thanksgiving was officially ruined. "I forgot to take it out yesterday. But I took it from the freezer early this morning. I put it in the bathtub to defrost in some water. Only, I forgot about it. So I turned the oven up really high to compensate for it not being defrosted fully, and now it's charred on the outside and frozen in the middle. I'm a terrible girlfriend."

"Hey, what's this? You are not a terrible girlfriend." He cupped the side of her face, turning her to face him.

"But I can't even make Thanksgiving dinner for you and your family."

"They're your family too now. And who said that you had to? Do you really think I care whether you can cook a turkey or not?"

"I'm guessing the answer is no?" she said.

"The answer is definitely no. And I will not have you saying that you're terrible at anything, understand me?" he said sternly. "If you hadn't already hurt yourself, I'd turn you over my knee for that."

"Yes, Daddy."

He turned her around so she faced him, placing his hands on either side of her hips. "Here is what is going to happen. You're going to have a nap while I find some food to serve for dinner."

"No, Daddy."

"Excuse me," he said in a low voice.

"I mean, I don't need a nap, Daddy. I just want to help you."

"You do need a nap, and it would help me if you got some rest. You look exhausted, baby girl. I don't know how I didn't see it before." He ran a finger along her cheek. "Have I not been paying enough attention? Have I been neglecting you?"

"Of course not!" she said hotly.

"I know at times I've been distracted. But I hope you know that you're the world to me."

The last bit of tension eased out of her as he told her that.

"You're the world to me too, Daddy."

"Good girl. Let's go find Ricky Rhino and get you into a onesie for your nap." He lifted her down and led her up the stairs to their bedroom. He helped her onto the bed on her back, handing her Ricky Rhino. She hugged her toy tightly before a pacifier was held to her lips. As she sucked, he quickly stripped her and then put a red, white, and green striped onesie on her.

"There you are, baby girl," he said as he tucked her into bed.

"Don't need a nap, Daddy," she mumbled around the pacifier.

"Sure you don't." He ran his fingers through her hair as she drifted off to sleep.

MARKOVICH SAT on the bed and stared down at Dahlia for several minutes. What would he do without her? Over these past few months, she'd been his rock in the storm.

It felt like his world had been turned on its axis. Galina's betrayal had hit him hard. How had he never seen what she was like? Pavel, well, he understood him more. He'd always been selfish. Although what he'd done to the Fox...

Markovich sighed. He understood why the Fox wanted nothing to do with him. He'd been tarred by association. But he'd never known about him. If he had, he would have fought with everything he had to get his father to take him in.

Instead, the Fox had been beaten by Pavel's men and left for dead, only to be found by D'yavol.

He shuddered. That man's reputation was one of a ruthless killer. Without remorse. Some might argue the Fox was the same, but Markovich had gotten to know the other man while he'd 'worked' for him. And while the Fox might have some issues with empathy and morality, he wasn't evil.

He wasn't an emotionless robot, like it was rumored that D'yavol was.

He'd tried several times to reach out to his half-brother. Shit, it was weird to think of the Fox as his brother, but nothing. Perhaps he should leave it alone now.

It was never a good idea to annoy an assassin.

9

Markovich and Dahlia

"I'm so sorry there's no turkey," Dahlia apologised, staring at the food on the table in dismay.

"Baby, stop apologizing," he commanded.

He'd had enough of her saying sorry. None of this was her fault. He should have had dinner catered. The truth was, he hadn't even thought about what they were going to eat, and that was on him.

While he'd lived in the USA for a long time, this wasn't a holiday that had any real meaning to him. But it did to Dahlia, so he had to make an effort.

"Don't stress, Dahlia. When I lived with Senior, we didn't even celebrate Thanksgiving. If I was lucky, the cook would sneak me some pumpkin pie from the meal she'd make for the staff left watching over me."

"Fuck," Reyes muttered at Emme's words. Reaching over, he grasped her around the back of the neck and drew her close to kiss her. "Damn, little girl, sometimes you kill me."

"I do? I don't want to do that, though," Emme replied.

"I hate what that bastard did to you," Reyes said with a scowl.

Markovich knew how he felt. He wished Senior was still alive, so he could be the one to kill him. Nice and slow.

"Oh no!" Dahlia cried. "I didn't even think about pumpkin pie! You never got to celebrate Thanksgiving, and now you have to eat lasagna and chicken casserole."

"But I like those things," Emme said quickly. "And I brought pumpkin pie for dessert.'"

"You did?" Dahlia asked, her face lighting up with hope.

"Uh-huh, don't worry, D. Everything is awesome."

"If we waited a few hours, the turkey might be ready. Dimitri put it back in the oven."

He sent her a surprised look. "Baby girl, I threw it out."

"What?" she asked. "Oh no! No turkey? At all?"

"I'll get you a new one," he said hastily, hating the look of sadness on her face. "I'll go find you one right now."

"No, no," she said with a sniffle. "I'm being silly. Sorry. It's just that it's our first Thanksgiving together . . . and I . . . I was trying to make it perfect, and instead, it ended up a disaster."

"Baby, come here." He patted his lap. He'd had enough of this.

Getting up, she moved slowly toward him. Reyes and Emme were quietly talking to each other as Reyes piled food onto Emme's plate. He drew Dahlia onto his lap.

"Baby girl, what is this all about?" he whispered in her ear.

"I just . . . I want . . ." She gave Reyes and Emme a look.

"Let's go talk about this in private."

A banging door made him jump. Reyes stood.

Fuck! Why didn't he have his gun on him?

"Hello! We're here!"

He knew that voice . . . but how the fuck had he gotten into the house without the guards alerting him?

"Emme, get down," Reyes ordered.

Markovich lifted Dahlia off his lap. "Dahlia, down with her."

"What is it? Who's here?" she asked.

"Now, baby."

He didn't have time for her questions. There was a gun in his sideboard. He didn't think their visitor was a threat, but the fact he'd turned up unannounced and gotten through his security . . . red flag.

He grabbed a gun from his sideboard as the man in question walked in, flinging open the doors to make a grand entrance.

There was a large smile on his face. "The party can start now that I'm here!" His gaze immediately shot to where Markovich was holding his gun at his side.

For some reason he felt guilty when he shouldn't.

"Really? Is this the way you greet your long-lost brother? A gun? That wounds me. Perhaps literally."

"You surprised me," Markovich added. They were staring at each other from across the room. The Fox eyed him coldly.

Fuck. Had he fucked this all up?

But what was he doing here?

"You practically get down on your knees and beg me to come visit you and this is how I'm treated?"

"I didn't know you were coming. You surprised me! And how did you get through security?"

"Pfft. That was simple. I knocked your guards out and used my passcode."

"You knocked them out? You've left us defenseless? And what passcode? You don't have a passcode!"

"Of course I do. I'm your brother. And the guards will wake

up soon. Don't be so precious. Besides, I have the place alarmed."

"You ... what ... how ..."

"I've had a system in place since before you contacted me about a job. Had to have a way in for when I decided to kill you."

Dahlia made a small noise and Markovich prayed the Fox didn't hear her. But he crouched down, smiling at the girls. "Hello, there. Are you playing a game of hide and seek? I don't think my Bunny would feel comfortable playing that in a strange house. She might get scared after everything she's been through. But my Pup might. Or at least he likes a game of the Big Bad Wolf. Although, what happens after isn't something I can do—"

"Fox!" Reyes snapped. "You can't talk about that."

"What? About how I like to have him present and—"

"Fox!" Markovich interrupted him this time. The other man didn't seem to like that, but the girls did not need to hear this.

None of them did.

"I was only going to say I spank him, kiss him, and then send him running again. Wow, you all have such filthy minds. You should get them examined. I can recommend an excellent therapist."

"You have a therapist?" Emme asked.

"Emme," Reyes warned.

He really wished she hadn't spoken as the Fox turned back to the girls.

"Ah, is that my niece? Isn't that weird? That you're my niece. I'm not sure how I feel about that yet. I mean ... if I start to feel like an uncle, then I might have to object to this guy being your fiancé." He pointed to Reyes.

"Hey, what's wrong with Reyes?" Emme asked.

"Hmm, what isn't wrong with him would probably be a shorter list."

"Fox," Markovich said, before Reyes' temper exploded. "Why are you here?"

"Rude. I'm here for Thanksgiving dinner, of course. You invited me."

He had.

Lord help him.

"You never replied."

"Family has to RSVP? Is that a rule?" he asked.

A rule? What did he mean?

"Thanksgiving dinner is ruined," Dahlia said, poking her head out.

"Dahlia," he said in a low voice. Oh, that girl was getting her butt reddened later. "I did not say you could move."

"Is this some sort of Thanksgiving tradition? For the women to hide under the table? Not sure I like the idea of that. My Bunny could hit her head. Actually, she would hit her head. She's a little clumsy."

"It's not a tradition. We had them hide down there because you snuck into the house," Reyes said in a dark voice.

Fuck. This was not how he'd expected today to go.

He'd been thinking it would be low-key. Just a dinner like the family dinners they tried to have once a week.

Instead . . . it was becoming something else.

"You think I'm a threat to your women?" The Fox drawled in a quiet voice. "My niece and the woman I kept safe when I warned you about the threat to her?"

"No," Markovich said quietly. As a sign of good faith, he returned his gun to the drawer. "No one thinks that."

"More fool you, then. I could be."

Fuck. Shit.

His heart slowed. Was this it? Was he here to avenge what Pavel had done to him when he was a child? He didn't blame the Fox. He just hoped he didn't take out on the girls.

"Fox," a quiet voice said.

Was someone else there?

"Brody?" Reyes asked.

"Luckily for you all, I've brought my babies with me. So there won't be any bloodshed. However, there might be two smacked bottoms when I get home tonight. I told the two of you to wait in the car."

"It was my fault," a feminine voice whispered. "I have to pee."

"You should have texted, Bunny. Markovich, toilet. My girl has to pee."

"Fox, you don't have to say it so loudly," she complained.

He couldn't see them yet. They had to be standing away from the door.

"Why are you concerned? I didn't tell them you had to poop."

"Fox," Brody groaned.

"Well, what other reason would you need the bathroom for?" the Fox reasoned.

Markovich had to smile. It had been hard for him to wrap his head around how the Fox could be a Daddy Dom. And that he had not just one Little but two.

"I have a bathroom," Markovich responded.

"Be worried if you didn't." The Fox was smiling wide, but Markovich knew him well enough to know that this wasn't necessarily his true persona. He wondered if anyone knew all of him. He guessed the two people who lived with him knew more than anyone else.

Markovich knew that he'd likely never fully know or understand him, but all he was asking was for a chance to know him better.

Although sometimes he'd wondered if that was a good idea.

"I'll show you where it is," he offered.

"Oh, don't bother, I know where it is. I'll take my babies. But

I must warn you, if any of you pull a gun with them in the room, I will make you regret it."

He knew where the bathroom was?

Fuck.

Of course he did. He had a damn passcode for the gate. He'd gotten in here without anyone alerting him.

The Fox disappeared, closing the door behind him. Markovich grabbed his phone, relieved as his guards answered. They sounded slightly groggy, but they were conscious and able to continue their jobs.

"You think we could come out from under the table now?" Emme asked. "I'm getting cramped."

"You're tiny, how are you cramped?" Reyes asked.

"I just am. Plus, the food is getting cold."

"Come on." Markovich moved forward and crouched, holding out his hand to Dahlia. She slid her hand into his and he helped her up.

"I can't believe the Fox turned up with two extra people and there's nothing to feed them," Dahlia said, clearly panicking. "This is a disaster."

"Hey, look at me," he said firmly. He cupped her face between his hands, tilting her face back. "He turned up unannounced, so he can't expect much. Okay?"

"Okay," she whispered. Although she didn't look all that convinced. She bit her lip and he reached up to release it, kissing her lightly.

The door opened again with a bang, making Dahlia jump.

"Goat's balls!" Emme cried. "You nearly made me pee myself."

"Do you need me to show you where the bathroom is?" the Fox asked her.

"No, she doesn't," Reyes told him.

"No need to be insulted. I was just trying to help."

Behind him, Brody stepped into the room. He was wearing a dark jacket and jeans which looked to have a stain on them. His hair was shaggy around his ears, and he nervously pushed his glasses back up his nose as he glanced around.

"Hey, Reyes, Emme, Dahlia, Markovich."

Hidden half behind Brody was a small woman. She peeked out, her eyes studying them all before she slid back. She had dark auburn hair that was pulled back into two pigtails. And she wore a white jacket with pictures of cherries on it.

"Brody," Reyes said. "Are you all right?"

"Yep, I'm good." Brody smiled and took off his jacket. Underneath he wore a T-shirt with the image of a turkey on it. The bird held a sign saying: Save a Turkey, Eat Pizza. "Sorry to turn up unexpectedly like this."

"It's okay," Dahlia said. "Here let me take that. And yours?" She stepped toward Autumn and suddenly, the Fox was between the two women.

"My Bunny is a bit shy. I'll help her."

Markovich frowned, worried Dahlia would be upset. That was going to cause problems.

No one upset his baby girl.

But Dahlia's face just softened. "That's okay. I get how hard it can be when you don't know anyone. But we're practically sisters."

The Fox turned to Autumn, unzipping her jacket before pulling it off. Markovich watched him in amazement. He'd never have thought the other man capable of caring for someone like that. And he did it all so gently.

Then he handed her jacket to Dahlia, who walked out with them. When she returned, she looked flushed as though she'd been running.

Markovich frowned and crooked a finger at her. He didn't

like her being far from him. After everything that had happened this year, he had to know she was close by.

"Were you running?" he asked.

"Just a little bit," Dahlia said guiltily.

"No running in the house. Especially since you hurt your legs. How are your shins?" He wrapped his arm around her.

She gave him an incredulous look. "They're fine. I think we have other things to deal with right now."

"Nothing is as important as you."

Her entire face softened. Did her eyes get teary? He knew something was up with her, he just couldn't work out what it was.

"You hurt yourself?" Emme asked. "What happened?"

"Nothing, it's nothing," Dahlia said.

It wasn't nothing, but he didn't push her.

"Sorry, we're late. Brody's family wouldn't let me leave. They adore me. Who wouldn't?" The Fox held out his arms. "So has all the food been eaten or are you still bringing it out?"

10

Markovich and Dahlia

Dahlia gaped at the Fox. He didn't look the same as the last time she'd met him. Today he had mousy brown hair and he seemed shorter too. Although maybe that was an illusion.

But the way he was acting . . . yeah, that was the man she'd met.

She tried to get a glimpse of the woman standing behind Brody, but she stayed hidden. She had to wonder how she was dealing with the Fox if she was so shy and quiet.

But perhaps that's why it worked since the Fox was so outspoken.

"I ruined Thanksgiving lunch!" Dahlia said. "The turkey was frozen, so I turned the oven up too high and burned the outside while the middle didn't get cooked at all. All I have is a sweet potato casserole and some cranberry sauce. Because that's all I didn't mess up. So we're eating lasagna and chicken casserole instead."

She tensed, waiting for what they'd say.

"I like lasagna."

It was Autumn who spoke. She stepped out from behind Brody, her hand held in his. "Brody-bear does too, don't you?"

"Sure do," Brody replied cheerfully.

Dahlia studied the food. Did they have enough?

"And we have leftovers, too," Autumn added.

"Duh, how did I forget? Idiot!" Brody smacked his hand against his forehead. "I'll go get them."

The Fox reached out to take hold of Brody's hand. "Don't hurt yourself. Or call yourself names."

Brody gulped, but nodded. To her surprise, the Fox leaned forward to lightly kiss Brody's lips. "I'll come with you to get the food."

The Fox left the room with both Brody and Autumn to get the food.

"Well," Emme said. "This was unexpected."

"You can say that again," Dahlia muttered. "Do we have enough dessert?"

"Doubtful. Hopefully, they brought some of that too," Emme replied.

"If we don't, we'll sort it out," Markovich reassured her.

To her shock, Brody entered carrying a stack of containers filled with food. It didn't take long for her and Emme to heat everything. When the food was all laid out, well, it was a feast.

Things were still a bit tense, however. She glanced at the Fox and then over to Dimitri. What was Dimitri thinking? This is what he'd wanted, but maybe not under these circumstances.

Then again . . . it was always going to be on the Fox's terms, wasn't it?

She watched as the Fox filled both Autumn and Brody's plates before his own. That was sweet.

That wasn't something she'd ever thought she'd think of the Fox.

"I really don't think I can eat this much," Autumn said, looking at her food with dismay.

The Fox whispered something to her that had her nodding and blushing.

"Okay, Daddy," she said back.

Or at least that's what Dahlia thought she said. It was hard to hear. She seemed so sweet, though. Dahlia would love to know her better.

"So . . . Fox, what made you come today?" Dimitri asked.

She shot the Fox a look, worried he might take offense. Or think they didn't want him here. It wasn't that . . . she knew this was what Dimitri had hoped for but didn't think would ever happen.

The Fox shrugged. "Figured I'd take pity on you. All that begging . . ."

"Fox," Brody said in a low voice.

Both Brody and Autumn were shooting the Fox chiding looks. Whoa, they were brave.

"Perhaps I am here because the idea of family isn't completely repugnant to me."

Whoa. That wasn't what she was expecting him to say.

"But don't get any ideas. We're not doing family dinners. There's to be no hugging. Or calling me when you break down on the side of the road to tow your car. Or to help when you move houses. I don't do any of that." The Fox pointed his fork at Markovich, then Emme.

She saw Reyes bristle. Shoot.

"We don't expect that, right, Dimitri?" she said.

The Fox grunted. "I suppose you could get the family and friends discount for my services."

"So if we need someone killed, you'll discount your fee?" Emme asked.

"Emme," Reyes said, staring down at her. "We won't need his services."

"With the lives you and your friends' lead, I wouldn't be so quick to say that," the Fox warned.

That was actually a fair call. Although, with Mr. X, Pavel, and Galina out of the way, hopefully things would be unexciting from now on. So far, so good.

"I was just wanting to know," Emme explained.

"For you, niece, it's a fifty percent discount. Any of your friends and Markovich, twenty percent off. For Reyes, I'll add ten percent."

"What? Why?" Emme asked.

"I don't like his face."

"Fox," Brody warned.

The Fox sighed long and loud. "Really? I can't say that?"

"It's kind of rude," Autumn said.

"Fine. All this social nicety stuff is trying, though. There's so much I can't say without offending delicate sensibilities."

She wasn't sure she was buying it. He had to know he was being rude. Was it on purpose? Maybe because he was more uncomfortable than he was letting on?

"Fine, Reyes, ten percent discount for you," the Fox told him.

"Thanks," Reyes said dryly.

"You're welcome."

He forked up some food from Autumn's plate and held it to her lips. The other woman blushed but let him feed it to her.

"We could have a playdate sometime," Dahlia blurted out. Then she felt herself growing red. "Sorry, sometimes I have no filter. Stuff just comes out."

"That's okay," Brody said kindly. "Maybe we could. I'll get my Daddy to talk to yours." He winked at her.

She blushed even harder, but was grateful to him.

"Perhaps," the Fox allowed. "If we come back."

She hoped they did. The Fox spooned up some sweet potato casserole. After putting it in his mouth, he made a weird face.

"Holy crap. What's in this?" He grabbed a napkin and spat it out.

"Oh no! Is it no good?" she asked. She quickly ate some, and her eyes nearly bulged out of her head. "Not good. Not good."

"What is it?" Markovich asked. He walked around and crouched beside her, holding her glass of water to her lips.

"It tastes awful!" she said. "I think I put too much vanilla extract in. I like vanilla so I thought I'd add more. I'm so sorry!"

"Hey, there's nothing to be sorry for. It doesn't matter," Markovich told her.

"I wish I hadn't fucked everything up. Idiot!"

There was a stunned silence.

"You going to let her talk about herself like that?" the Fox asked curiously.

"This is between Dahlia and me," Dimitri snapped back.

Oh no, she didn't want them fighting.

But the Fox seemed to approve of his words as he nodded slowly. "Probably hard on her. I imagine she's thinking of all the ways she's different from Galina. I mean, there's the obvious . . . she's not a scheming, conniving, murderous bitch. But was Galina a good cook? Maybe she wasn't. I don't know."

Emme sucked in a breath, and Dimitri looked at her in concern.

"It's okay . . . she was those things," Emme said quietly. "I didn't know her, so it doesn't hurt as much for me."

"Dahlia?" Markovich asked.

"I . . . um . . . what would you have done?" she asked. "If she'd come back, and she wasn't like . . . like what she was . . . who would you have chosen?"

The words were out before she could take them back. His mouth dropped open in shock.

Whoops.

Maybe she shouldn't have just come out with that question like that.

"Baby," he whispered.

"I think it's time we left," Brody said.

"Yes, I think it is," Reyes agreed.

She turned to see them all getting up. "Oh no, I'm sorry. I didn't mean to send you all away."

Emme rushed around and hugged her hard. "You haven't. Honestly, this is the best Thanksgiving I've ever had."

She knew the other woman was lying. This had been so bad.

"Thank you for having us," Autumn said quietly.

"It was lovely to meet you. I'm sorry," she replied.

"Don't be," Brody said. "We barged in. Maybe next time we can let you know when we're coming first."

"Will there be another time?" she asked. She'd like to see them all again. Even the Fox. If he and Dimitri could sit down for a proper conversation . . .

"Will you come back?" Dimitri asked, standing.

The Fox looked at Autumn then Brody. "Well, I suppose I could think about it. It's been interesting . . . and I like interesting. It definitely hasn't been boring. I hate being bored."

They were all gone before she could catch her breath. Dimitri turned and held out his hands to her. "Come with me."

"I have to clean up, though. I can't leave all this food out here." She stood and started grabbing plates. But he took them from her, putting them down on the table.

"Dahlia," he said warningly. "Come with me."

She slid her hand into his and he led her into his office.

Uh-oh.

Was she about to get her butt spanked? But when he sat on the sofa, he drew her down to sit on his lap. Then he just held her. Gradually, her body relaxed, the tension draining from her.

Grasping hold of her chin, he turned her face to his and kissed her. "I'm sorry."

"What . . . what are you sorry for?"

"For not making it perfectly clear how much you mean to me. For being too far inside my own head to see that you were struggling."

"No. I'm not . . . I'm not struggling, Dimitri," she reassured him. "I know you love me. It's just sometimes, I start thinking about the 'what ifs'. I know it's stupid. It didn't happen. So what does it matter?"

"It matters if it upsets you. Look at me."

She glanced up at him.

"I love you. Dahlia, you're my entire world. You're the one I want by my side, in my bed, and my life. In fact . . ." He lifted her off his lap and then stood, moving to his safe, which was hidden in the floor.

When he returned, he held a velvet box in his hand. Tears dripped down her cheeks.

"Daddy," she whispered as he got down on his knees in front of her.

He took hold of her left hand in his. "L'venok, I think you're amazing. You're sweet and funny. Kind and caring. Brave and resourceful. Sometimes too brave. I swear you've given me more gray hair since I've known you. But I know that you will always do what you think is right. And that it's up to me to protect you while you do that. I don't want you to ever worry about what I think of you or whether I want you because when I met you, I knew you were mine and that I would never let you go. No. Matter. What."

"Really?" she whispered.

"I once loved Galina. She gave me my Zvezda. But what I felt for her . . . it faded a long time ago. It seems I never really knew her fully, so I was in love with an illusion. And I won't lie . . . I have struggled with that. With missing her true nature. Although I think she grew more depraved and bitter over the years. But what we had? It was my past. And it would have been the past no matter what. Maybe that makes me sound harsh. But you are my present and my future. You, Dahlia. No one else."

He drew back his hand to open the box. She stared down at the enormous solitaire diamond on a rose gold band.

"Dahlia, will you do this old man the honor of being my wife? Of being my Little, my love, for the rest of my life and beyond?"

"Yes, Dimitri! Yes!" She threw herself at him and he held onto her tight with one arm.

"Let me get this on you before you change your mind."

"I will never change my mind, Daddy." But she drew back and held out her left hand.

He slid the ring onto her finger.

Perfect fit.

"Oh, Dimitri. It's beautiful."

"Like you."

She wrapped herself around him, kissing him longingly. Standing, he drew her up with him. He pulled back, staring down at her. She let out a small sound of protest. "It was naughty of you to keep your worries from me, baby girl."

She stuck her lip out in a pout. "But, Daddy—"

"And don't think I didn't notice the Christmas decorations. How did you get those up so high?"

"Oh, um, well . . . I got on a ladder," she confessed.

"Are you allowed on ladders?"

"No, Daddy."

"I can see I've been neglecting you."

Her mouth dropped open. "No, Daddy!"

"No? I think yes. You put yourself at risk and didn't come to me when something was worrying you. That's going to be a count of twenty."

"But we just got engaged!"

"Yes, but we should start as we mean to go on. And you should be grateful I'm not spanking you for running in the house. Now, you're to strip off all your clothes and go stand in the corner. Bottom out, legs spread."

She sighed forlornly. "Yes, Daddy."

11

Markovich and Dahlia

MARKOVICH STARED at his girl as she stood facing the corner.

His dick was hard, pressing against his pants. Sometimes, she made him feel eighteen again. All he wanted was to lay her down on the floor, eat her out until she screamed, and then take her until she was under no illusions about who owned her.

Him.

Now that he understood what had been going on inside her mind, he was angry at himself for not figuring it out earlier. Of course, Galina coming back was going to affect her. He just hadn't realized what the problem had been.

And in a way, he had the Fox to thank for it all coming out.

He sighed. He didn't know how he felt about him turning up for dinner. It hadn't been easy. It hadn't felt like some family reunion with warm fuzzies. But then, neither he nor the Fox could really be described as warm men.

But perhaps they could find a way to connect, even if it was just through their Littles. He pushed the Fox from his mind. Right now, he had his girl to deal with.

"Come here, baby girl."

She turned, rubbing her finger under her nose, something she often did when she was nervous. Didn't she know she didn't have to be nervous around him? As she moved closer, he drew her onto his lap, holding her tight.

"Hey, you don't have to be scared or nervous of me."

"I know, Daddy." She sighed, slumping against him.

"If you don't want this, just tell me no."

"No, I think I'll feel better after. I need this."

"Good girl for telling me what you need." He arranged her over his lap. "Now, the count is twenty. Are you ready?"

"Yes, Daddy."

He didn't waste time. The spanks landed steadily. It didn't take long for her skin to turn pink.

About six spanks in, she started kicking her feet and protesting.

"Daddy, please!"

"I'm sorry," he said. "But we're not even halfway through."

As she started sobbing, he had to harden his heart. She needed to know that he took her safety seriously. She could have fallen from that ladder.

And that she should tell him when something worried her. He never wanted her to stress over anything. But especially anything that concerned their relationship.

His poor baby. He finished up her spanking, her ass hot and red. Placing his hand on her bottom, he held her there for a few moments longer.

"Are you going to climb any more ladders?"

"N-no, Daddy," she sobbed.

"And are you going to keep things from me that are worrying you?"

"N-no, Daddy."

He drew her over, so she was straddling his lap. Then he hugged her tight, rubbing her back. "Good girl. Shh. You're my good girl. Just let it all out."

Finally, she pulled back and he grabbed his handkerchief from his pocket, wiping away her tears and holding it to her nose so she could blow it. He set it down and brushed his fingers lightly through her hair.

"Sorry I was naughty," she said. "And that I kept stuff from you. I just didn't know that I wanted to know the answer to my questions."

"Well, now you know the answer." He drew back, cupping her face. "The answer is always you."

12

Fox, Brody, and Autumn

Autumn shook Brody awake. He let out a snort, then slapped at her hands. "No, don't wanna go to school today."

"Brody-bear, wake up!" She shook him again.

Opening his eyes, he scowled at her. He was such a deep sleeper that he never reacted well when he was woken up.

But this was important.

"Tutu? That you?" He blinked up at her.

She grabbed his glasses and handed them to him. He put them on, then sat up. "What is it? What's wrong? Did you have a nightmare?"

"Nuh-uh, it's Christmas!"

"What?" He turned and glanced at the clock. "It's two in the morning. I am not getting up to open presents."

He lay back, his eyes already closing.

"All right, seems like I'm going to catch a Santa on my own." She stood and moved to the doorway.

"What did you say?" he whispered.

Turning, she saw he was sitting up in bed. He threw back the covers and got up. He was wearing the same Christmas pajamas as she was. She'd ordered them online for the three of them. They all had white tops and red and black checked pants. But they each had different sayings on the front.

Brody's shirt said: Ring My Bells and I'll Show You a White Christmas.

He'd been a bit horrified when she'd given it to him. But she and the Fox had cracked up.

Her top said: I'm So Good, Santa Came Twice.

And the Fox's had an image of a candy cane and said: It's Not Going To Lick Itself.

"Tutu? What are you doing?"

"I'm going to catch myself a Santa." She picked up the giant fishing net she'd ordered online for just this purpose. "Hopefully, a Foxy Santa."

Brody groaned. "You're gonna get us in so much trouble."

"You don't have to come with me."

"Like I'm going to let you go alone."

She took hold of his hand and they both creeped out toward the living room. They had an enormous tree that the Fox had chopped down himself. That had been so sexy. She'd wanted to get down on her knees and suck him off then and there. But he'd made her wait until they got back into the den.

Such fun.

Hmm, seemed the Fox might be rubbing off on her.

The enormous tree was lit up with Christmas lights, which meant they could easily spot the man filling their Christmas stockings and placing presents under the tree.

He had a huge red sack. And he was dressed in red pants and

a coat. He even had a large tummy. For a moment, she thought it might really be Santa.

Then he turned, piercing them with a look that was all Fox. She squealed, drew her net up, and put it down over his head. He stared at her, shocked.

"I caught you, Santa!"

"Oh dear Lord. We're never going to sit again," Brody muttered.

She giggled like a maniac. "Now he has to grant all our wishes, Brody-bear."

Brody turned to her. "He's not a genie."

"What?"

"A genie grants wishes. Santa comes down your chimney with presents."

"And do you know what a Foxy Santa does?" the Fox said. Reaching up, he grabbed the net, tossing it aside.

Autumn squealed. Brody backed away, taking her with him.

"What?"

"He chases down naughty Little boys and girls and spanks their bottoms."

Turning, they raced off. She was laughing so hard she could barely see anything. She banged her knee against the wall but kept running.

"Be careful," the Fox ordered. "No hurting yourself."

He sounded like he was right behind them. . . she screamed as she found herself flying through the air. She was twisted before she landed over the Fox's shoulder. He walked with her back to their bedroom, smacking her ass as he sang, Bunny Got Her Bottom Smacked to the tune of *Grandma Got Run Over by a Reindeer* as he walked and spanked.

Damn him for being one of the few men who could multi-task.

When he got to their bedroom, he set her on her feet and

pointed to the corner. "In you go. I want your bare butt on display."

She rubbed her poor butt. His spanks stung!

"Daddy, that's not fair. It was just a bit of fun."

"Oh no, I'm not Daddy right now. I'm Foxy Santa. I'm much stricter than Daddy."

Gulp.

"Now, do as you were told. I have to find your accomplice."

Poor Brody. He'd been right. She had gotten him in big trouble.

There was a noise about five minutes later, and she turning her head, her eyes widened as she took in Brody. He was over the Fox's shoulder and his pajama pants were already down at his ankles as the Fox steadily spanked him.

"Papa!" he complained. "Those spanks hurt."

"They were meant to. I'm not Papa right now. I'm Foxy Santa. Into the corner with you. Ass out."

"I think he thinks he's really Santa," she whispered to Brody.

"No talking! Or you get extras. Now I have to go swap all your gifts for coal."

"No, please, Daddy! I mean, Foxy Santa. Don't take our gifts," she begged.

"I suppose if you accept your punishment without complaint, then go back to sleep, I won't have to swap out your gifts."

"We promise, Foxy Santa," she said.

"Uh-huh, we promise," Brody said.

"All right. I'll get the special gifts I have for you."

Special gifts. Uh-oh. She didn't know if she liked the sound of that.

THE FOX WALKED BACK into the bedroom, carrying his sack. He'd known that sneaking out to catch him would be too much for his Bunny to resist, which is why he'd gotten all dressed up.

And he'd left a couple of gifts inside his sack.

And no, he wasn't talking about his balls. Ha-ha.

He placed the gifts on the bed and switched on the light on the nightstand before pulling each gift out.

"Both of you strip off then come here," he ordered his naughty babies.

After taking off their pajamas, they turned and walked over to him. Pup reached out and took his Bunny's hand in his.

"Kneel." He sat on the bed next to the gifts.

"Open this one first, Bunny." He handed her a smaller gift.

She opened it slowly, gaping down at it. "Gingerbread lube?"

"Yep. Always important to have lube."

"Oh heck," Brody said.

"Don't worry, Pup. I have a gift for you too." He handed him one next.

Brody opened it, revealing a red cock ring with a small bell hanging off the end.

"Let's just take care of that now, shall we? Stand up."

With a groan, Brody stood. The Fox placed a bit of lube on the inside of the ring, then he put it over Brody's dick, situating it at the base.

"Now, let's just make sure this is in the right place and isn't hurting you." The Fox slid his mouth over his Pup's dick.

It didn't take long before his Pup's cock grew erect, until he was panting and shaking.

Perfect.

The Fox pulled back, looking down at his dick. "Good boy. Kneel."

As he kneeled down, the bell jingled.

"Oh, that's just terrible," Autumn said. "I love it."

He had to grin.

"Next gift." He held it out to her.

She opened it eagerly. Poor girl. She gasped as she saw the Frosty paddle that was revealed. It was made of plastic and not very strong, he certainly wouldn't be spanking hard.

After all, he didn't really want to punish them. This was just a bit of fun.

"Right, let's make sure this works, shall we?" he said.

"Frosty can't spank my butt-butt, Daddy!" Autumn protested.

"Uh-uh, I'm not Daddy, remember?"

"Please, Foxy Santa." She pouted.

"I'm sorry," he said, pretending a reluctance he didn't feel. "But Foxy Santa says you were naughty getting out of bed and trying to capture him. And remember, it's this, or you lose your presents."

"We can do this, Tutu," Pup told her.

"Fine. Mean Frosty."

"You're going to bend over the edge of the bed and stick your bottoms out. Here is a pillow for your knees." He handed them one pillow each and they placed it under their knees before leaning over the bed. He stood and walked behind them.

"Just beautiful. I don't know how your Daddy doesn't spank your asses every day. I'll mention it to him."

"No," Autumn cried. He smacked the paddle down on her bottom. Then on Brody's bottom.

It made a heck of a noise, but he'd already tested it on himself and knew how hard to hit. Back and forth he went, smacking the paddle on their bottoms. Once their cheeks were pink, he put the paddle back on the bed.

"You can sit back now."

They moved. Bunny was rubbing her bottom. Brody's erection was still thick and firm. Perfect.

"Last gift. I'll open this one."

"I don't think I want it," Bunny said, pouting.

"Don't be like that. You might like this one."

He picked up the last gift and opened it. They'd come in a box originally, but he'd had to get rid of that because of his Bunny's phobia of boxes.

Bunny's eyes widened as she saw the two items inside. "Wow, Daddy! Glass candy canes. Those are so pretty." She reached out a hand to run her finger over them. "What do you do with them? If you hang them on the tree they might fall and shatter."

"I don't think you hang them in your tree, Tutu," Brody said, looking up at him knowingly.

"No? Then what do you do? They don't look like they stand on their own. I guess you could put them out as a table decoration. On a plate or something. That would be cute."

"You definitely don't display them out on a plate," the Fox told her.

"Then what?" She looked from him to Brody. "What are they?"

"They're plugs, Tutu," Brody explained, taking pity on her.

"Plugs . . . these wouldn't plug the sink. Oh my God! They're not that sort of plug, are they?"

"Nope," the Fox replied. "These here are anal plugs."

She winced. "They go in your bottom?"

"Well, not my bottom. But your bottom and Pup's, yes."

"I don't know, Daddy, I mean, Foxy Santa. I think they're too pretty to go up anyone's bottom."

"I think you'll look extra pretty with a nice red bottom and the top of the candy cane sticking out."

"Dear Lord, that's just depraved," Brody told him.

"It certainly is." He grinned. "Now, I want you both to stand and then bend right over. I need to get you ready with the gingerbread lube."

. . .

As Autumn bent over, she thought that perhaps it hadn't been a wise idea to sneak out and try to catch Santa.

Then again . . . this was kind of fun too. Although she could have done without Frosty spanking her butt.

She could hear him rustling around. What was he doing? Prepping the plugs? Oh Lord, was he going to plug them while they stood here like this?

So. Embarrassing.

"Both of you reach back and part your butt cheeks."

She let out a small squeak. Really? She glanced at Brody, but he'd already reached his arms back. He winked at her, and she let out a deep breath before pulling her butt cheeks apart.

Suddenly, she felt some damp fingers at her back hole. There was a tingling sensation as the Fox pushed two fingers into her hole. Whoa, that gingerbread lube packed a punch.

"Foxy Santa, that feels weird. It's kind of hot."

"It's meant to be a little . . . spicy."

Good. Lord. Then his fingers slipped free and something hard and cool was pressed against her back hole.

"Daddy? I mean, Foxy Santa?"

"Breathe out. You can do this. This is far, far, far smaller than me. It should just slip right on in."

Slip right on in.

Right. She'd like to see if it would slip right on into his butt.

"How come we never get to plug you, Daddy?"

"Because I'm the Daddy," he replied. "Well, not right now. I'm Foxy Santa."

Right. As if that answered everything. Although . . . she guessed in some ways it did.

He pushed the plug inside her as she breathed out. It felt so hard.

"It's cold, Foxy Santa," she complained, even though it had already grown warmer.

"I could have put it in the freezer," he told her, patting her bottom lightly.

"Are you going to take it back out, Daddy?" she asked. She could only imagine how it looked.

"Oh no, you're going to stay right where you are with that plug sticking out of your bottom. You can let go of your bottom cheeks, though."

Great.

"Thank you so much," she said sarcastically.

"You're welcome," he replied seriously. "Pup, you're next."

"I'm ready, Foxy Santa."

"That's my good boy."

She wished she could see what he was doing. She loved watching them together.

"There you are, Pup. You've taken your plug so well. Good Pup."

She felt the Fox move back and shifted from foot to foot when she heard some water run.

"Stay still, baby girl."

"But, Foxy Santa, what were you doing?" she asked.

"I was washing my hands and now I'm staring at my little candy canes. So cute. I saw these reindeer vibrators as well. I thought I might get one of those too. Just imagine the reindeer ears against your clit while you're plugged with this glass candy cane. Would you like that, baby girl?"

Her breath hitched. "I ... um ... "

"Tell me," he pressed.

"Yes, Foxy Santa."

"Good girl for being honest."

Darn, she loved when he called her a good girl. It made a shiver go up her spine.

His hand ran over her bottom then down between her legs. "Does that excite you, baby girl?"

"Yes," she managed to get out, knowing he'd find the evidence of her excitement.

He ran a finger through her drenched lips, circling her clit.

"I can tell you're very excited. What about you, Pup? Let's check." He removed his hand from her pussy and she bit her bottom lip to hold back her moan of disappointment.

She heard Brody groan and tried to glanced over. She caught glimpses of the Fox standing at Brody's side, running his hand up and down his cock.

She licked her lips. "Can I help you, Foxy Santa?"

"You want to suck Pup's cock, baby girl?"

"Ooh, yes, please."

Brody made another strangled noise.

"I bet you'd like that. And so would Pup. Unfortunately, this is a punishment, and neither of you gets to play."

That was so unfair. She was so turned on. Being plugged, having him touch her, watching him touch Brody . . . he was killing her. She'd almost forgotten the heat in her ass.

"Foxy Santa, please," she begged.

"No, baby girl. You can beg all you want, but you don't get to come or have Brody's cock in your mouth."

So. Mean.

The Fox slowly slid the plug from her ass and helped her stand before doing the same with Brody. "Both of you wait there while I wash these and my hands."

He disappeared into the bathroom and she leaned against Brody. "Do you think he's really serious about not letting us come?" Her poor clit was throbbing.

"He's serious."

"I need some relief, though. Or I'm gonna die!" Overdramatic? Not. At. All.

"You're going to die, huh? Well, how do you think I feel? Look at me."

They both glanced down at his erect cock.

"Darn, that's such a waste, Brody-bear."

"Uh-huh."

"If the two of you are finished mourning Pup's erection, it's time for a little Pup and Bunny to go to sleep. Get yourselves back into bed. Don't bother with your pajamas. Your Daddy will be back soon."

13

Fox, Brody, and Autumn

Brody lay back in bed with a groan.

At least Foxy Santa had removed the cock ring. It was made of rubber, so he'd just stretched it and pulled it off. But it didn't mean that his dick wasn't throbbing and hard.

Crap.

How was he going to go to sleep with this?

"I'm sorry I got us into trouble, Brody-bear."

He rolled to face Autumn. "Don't worry. I enjoyed every minute of it. I'm just suffering slightly now."

"I could help you."

"We'd get in more trouble," he warned.

"Could be worth it."

He grinned. "All right then." He moved onto his back as she

slid down the bed and put her mouth around his dick. Oh heck. Sugar balls. That felt so good.

He moaned.

"I see you've started without me."

Brody glanced over to see the Fox standing in the doorway. Naked.

His eyes widened. "Are you mad?"

Tutu drew the blankets back off her, then turned, letting him pop free while she turned to look at the Fox.

"Mad? Why would I be mad?"

"Because we were naughty and snuck down to catch Foxy Santa," Tutu said.

"Whatever happened between you and Foxy Santa stays between you," the Fox replied. "Now, did I say you could stop sucking off our boy?"

"No, Daddy."

"Then get to work."

Tutu turned, putting her mouth back on his cock while the Fox kneeled beside her, impaling her with one stroke. She cried out in pleasure. His arousal grew.

"I'm so close!" he cried.

"You'll wait for me, Pup." The Fox held Tutu by her hips, thrusting in and out of her pussy.

She moaned again and he noticed the Fox had moved one hand around to play with her clit.

"Fuck, you feel so good, Bunny," the Fox told her. "So wet and hot. Baby girl, you're killing me."

"You should feel her mouth," Brody said, panting. "My balls are aching. Please, Sir."

"Just a bit more, Pup. Fuck. I'm almost there. Are you nearly there, Bunny?"

She slid her mouth off Brody's dick. "Nearly, Daddy."

"Both of you are to come when I say. Get ready. Hell's bells. Fuck. You have no idea how good you feel, Bunny. How hot it is watching you suck on my boy. Come now. Come for me, my babies."

Brody groaned as Tutu took him deep, swallowing him down as he came. Tutu moaned around his cock while the Fox let out a loud shout and he followed them over.

Breathing heavily, Brody reached down for Autumn as she slid her mouth away from his dick. The Fox pulled back and grabbed her, drawing her up and then situating himself between them. He drew them both close, kissing their foreheads.

"Merry Christmas to me."

14

Fox, Brody, and Autumn

"Are you sure you told them we're coming, Daddy?" Autumn asked from the backseat.

"Of course I did," he replied.

"You did?" Brody asked, sounding skeptical as they pulled into a cute neighborhood. The houses were on the smaller side, but were situated on large plots of land and looked like they were well taken care of. The Fox drove into a driveway of a cute house that was painted white with a small porch at the front.

"Well, I didn't have to. I have an open invitation. And remember, it's not a party until the Fox walks in the door."

She groaned. So he hadn't told them. Awesome. It was going to be Thanksgiving all over again. And that had been kind of a disaster. Although, the Fox had agreed to see Markovich again sometime.

So there was that.

"I don't think they're here," she said, peering out the window. The house didn't look like there was anyone in it.

"Oh, this isn't their house. It's mine," the Fox replied.

"You own this house?" she asked.

"You sound like you don't believe me," he said. He hit something on his phone and the garage door went up.

"No, it's just, you know, not underground."

He snorted. "I bought it so I had a place to park, put in some surveillance, and be close by if needed."

He really did care about Sunny. She wondered if she should be jealous. But no, she knew Sunny was like his sister. A sister he guarded zealously and would murder anyone who dared to harm her.

But still . . . a sister.

"Wait, that's why you said they didn't want us to bring anything?" Brody asked. "Because they don't know we're coming?"

"Exactly." He didn't drive into the garage. Instead, he was doing something on his phone. "But you don't have to worry. We're not empty-handed, her present is due to be delivered soon."

"People deliver on Christmas?" Brody asked.

"They do if you pay them enough."

"What are you doing?" she asked.

"Checking cameras. Looks all okay, and the alarms haven't sounded." He drove in, turned off the car, and shut the door behind them. "Wait here, though."

Getting out, he entered the house.

Autumn undid her seatbelt, leaning forward. "Should you text Duke?"

Brody sighed. "At this stage, I think it wouldn't make any difference."

"True." She sighed.

"Everything okay, Tutu?" Brody asked in concern.

"Oh yeah, I'm just sad that there's no snow. It's Christmas Day! There should be snow."

"Poor Tutu."

The Fox came back for them, opening first Brody's door and helping him out. Then he opened her door. He frowned down at her. "You unlocked your own belt."

"Sorry, Daddy. Hugs?" She threw herself at him. He took a step back to balance himself, but held her against him, pulling her around onto his hip. "I think we should get you a harnessed seat."

Oh great.

After putting her down, he led the way through the house. It was fully furnished and looked nice, but you could tell it wasn't lived in. They went out through the front door. The Fox was on high alert, and she slipped her hand into Brody's as they followed him down along the sidewalk. They had to walk down a few blocks until they reached another charming house.

Wow, this is not where she expected a tattoo artist and member of a motorcycle club to live.

"This is their place. Sav and Livvy live next door," Brody explained. "I've been here once with Ink."

She nodded and tightened her hold on his hand as they walked up to the front door. The Fox drew a key out of his pocket.

"Fox, we should knock," Brody said.

"Where's the fun in that?" the Fox asked.

"Daddy, please."

He sighed. "Fine. But how am I supposed to mess with Duke if you guys won't let me have any fun? Then again, I guess I can save that surprise for another day."

Good. Lord.

They'd be lucky if Duke didn't shoot him on sight.

"Both of you wait around the corner. In case Duke is feeling frisky."

The Fox didn't sound at all worried about that. She and Brody stood off to the side of the house as the Fox knocked. A dark truck drove past as they stood there, slowing down slightly. She frowned. But it kept moving. Maybe the driver was lost.

"Hello?" a deep voice asked. "Can I help you?"

Oh, right. They wouldn't know it was Fox.

"Duke! I'm insulted. Don't you recognize me? And I thought we were the best of friends! Although you didn't ask me to be your best man at your wedding, which was rather insulting. Of course, I am more on Sunny's side of the family."

"Fox," the man hissed, his voice going from disinterested to annoyed.

Great. She cringed. She didn't want to stay if they weren't wanted.

Brody wrapped his arm around her shoulders. "If you're uncomfortable, we can leave."

"Aren't you going to invite us in?" the Fox asked. "My babies are getting cold."

"Your . . . babies."

"Who's there?" a woman called out.

"Merry Christmas, sweet girl," the Fox said.

"Fox! You're here. You came."

"You were expecting him?" Duke asked.

"I'm always kind of expecting him. He always turns up when you least expect him to. Hmm, I'm saying expect a lot. Come in. Wait, did you bring Brody and Autumn?"

"I did."

"Where are they?"

"They're right here." The Fox stepped back and gestured to them. She stepped around with Brody prodding her.

A big, dark-haired man frowned down at them both. He looked intimidating, although his face seemed to soften slightly as he took her in.

The woman beside him had dark-blonde hair pulled back in a high pony-tail. She was wearing pajama pants with candy canes on them. Her T-shirt featured a unicorn with rhinestones on its horn.

"Duke! Why did you leave them outside in the cold?" She lightly smacked the big man's arm.

"Yeah, Duke, why'd you leave us to freeze outside?" the Fox said.

"God help me," Duke muttered. "Please, come inside."

They walked in.

"Give me your coats," Sunny said. "I have some hot chocolate made and oh, no! I'm in my movie-watching clothes. I'm so sorry! I wasn't expecting anyone, not that you're not welcome. You are! I just . . . I need to go change and—"

"Little Rebel, you're fine," Duke rumbled.

"Please don't get changed," Brody added. "We barged in unannounced and besides, your outfit is cute."

Autumn nodded.

"Oh, well, it is comfy."

Duke looked Brody over as though searching for injury. Today, he wore a T-shirt that said: I'm Only A Morning Person At Christmas.

"You okay, man?" Duke asked.

"I do know how to take care of my Pup," the Fox said warningly.

"Come in, you're so welcome. Right, Duke?" Sunny said, ushering them into the living room. There was a movie paused on the television and the tree was a giant pink monstrosity decorated with unicorns. It was . . . like nothing she'd seen before.

"Sure." Then he turned to look at her and wiped the grimace off his face. "Hey, I'm Duke."

"And I'm Sunny." She waved at Autumn.

"This is Autumn," Brody said, clasping her hand tight. "She can be a bit shy sometimes."

"I . . . it's nice to meet you. Sorry, we didn't call ahead." She glared up at the Fox who raised his eyebrows.

"I don't . . . we've already eaten. Would you like some leftovers, though? I mean . . . we can eat again, right, Daddy?" Sunny said. "I mean, Duke. Sorry, I'm flustered. I just . . . I never thought I'd get to meet you, Autumn. Or that . . . that you'd be here like this." She glanced at the Fox. Tears filled her eyes.

"What's wrong? Why are you crying?" the Fox asked in alarm. He took hold of her arms. "Is it Duke? Tell me. I'll kill him right now."

"It . . . it's not Duke, Fox!" Sunny jumped in front of Duke, who was staring down at her, dumbfounded.

"Sunny!" Duke said sharply. "You don't ever get between me and danger."

"Sorry, Daddy. I just . . . he's not going to hurt me."

"My sweet girl is right. I'd never harm her. But did you hurt her?" the Fox said in a low voice.

"I would never harm her and you know it," Duke said warningly.

"I was just tearful because I'm happy," Sunny explained. "I like that you're able to be here as you . . . well, in disguise, but still you."

She knew it was a disguise?

"I just want this to work. Could this work? For a while at least, could we all get along?" Sunny asked hopefully. "For me?"

"Whoa, she's good," Brody whispered.

She so was.

"Of course, Little Rebel," Duke said reluctantly.

"I always get along with everyone," the Fox claimed. "It's one of my greatest charms. It's also a downfall when I have to kill someone. They get a bit pissed off at me. It's really a curse being this likeable."

Sunny just smiled at him. "Would you guys like something to drink?"

Another knock on the door interrupted them before they could answer and Duke moved to the door with a frown. "Who the fu-fudge could that be?"

"Oh, now the fun part starts. Come along. All of you put your jackets back on. Sweet girl, you need shoes too." The Fox ushered them toward the door as they saw a man leave and walk over to a truck. He opened up the back of it and let down a ramp.

"What is going on?" Sunny asked.

Duke turned to the Fox, a resigned look on his face. "You bought her the Maserati, didn't you?"

They all stared in shock as the man drove a bright pink Maserati down the ramp.

"It's beautiful," Sunny breathed. "Whose is it?"

"Why, yours of course, my sweet girl. You needed some new wheels."

"Fox, you didn't!"

"Of course I did. Who else would have?" the Fox asked.

"Fox," Duke groaned.

"I love it, but I can't accept it," Sunny said after the Fox accepted the keys from the delivery man, who put the ramp up then left. Probably eager to get home for the rest of the holiday.

"Why not?"

"It's too much. I can't. It wouldn't be right. But thank you for the thought." She threw herself at the Fox, hugging him.

He patted her back lightly.

"But I don't want it," the Fox said. "I have enough cars."

She shook her head, looking sad. "No, I can't."

"What if it was a wedding gift?" Autumn suggested.

They all turned to stare at her.

Brody smiled. "Yeah, you can't say no to a wedding gift, and then it's for both of you."

"But our wedding was ages ago, and the Fox gave me a gorgeous charm."

"Ahh, but that wasn't a gift for both of you," Brody said.

"Right, because I'm going to be driving a pink Maserati around a lot," Duke said dryly.

"Hey, what have you got against Maseratis?" the Fox asked.

"Nothing," Duke replied.

"Then is it the color?" Brody asked.

"Pink is an awesome color," Autumn argued.

"Yes," Sunny said. "Pink is an awesome color. Autumn gets it."

"I love your T-shirt, by the way," she said to Sunny. There was just something about the other woman that put her at ease. She hadn't felt like this around anyone other than Brody and the Fox in a long time.

"Aww, thank you. I love unicorns and rhinestones."

"You know, you'd hurt my feelings if you didn't take the car," the Fox said. "And no one wants to hurt my feelings."

They really didn't.

Duke groaned. "Fine. But this is the last gift, Fox. I mean it."

"Sure, of course it is." The Fox just grinned.

Oh, he was terrible.

Duke scowled, obviously understanding that the Fox would do whatever the hell he liked. "The girls and Brody need to get inside where it's warm."

Brody took her hand in his with a wink.

That same dark truck drove toward them. The Fox stiffened and moved to cover them. They all watched as it drove into the driveway next door. A dark-haired man with tattoos and a leather jacket got out. He looked like a badass.

"Who is that?" Sunny said.

"I don't know," Duke replied. "Let's get you inside. I'll text Sav." He had his phone out as soon as they were inside. They all took off their jackets and Sunny grabbed both her and Brody's hands. "Want to see my playroom?" There was a shy note to her voice.

Autumn looked over at Brody. "Yes, please."

Sunny's playroom was amazing. Ten minutes later, she and Sunny were sitting at the table and chairs drinking tea with Freddy Fox and Moody the monkey. Brody-bear was their butler.

"Oh, butler," Autumn said.

"Yes, ma'am?" Brody-bear said in a terrible British accent.

"Could you pour me some more tea? And I'll take more of the pink cookies."

"Certainly, ma'am."

"What sort of accent is that supposed to be?" the Fox asked from the doorway.

Sunny gave a startled gasp, but Autumn had known he was there. It was like a sixth sense or something.

A Foxy sense.

"It's a British one, Papa," Brody-bear said.

"That's terrible, Pup. Remind me to give you some lessons."

"Daddy, you can be our butler. Brody-bear needs some tea. Chop-chop."

"Chop-chop?" the Fox asked in a low drawl. "Is that really the way you speak to me, baby girl?"

"You're not you, Daddy. You're Butler Daddy. What goes on with Butler Daddy stays with Butler Daddy."

"I don't think I like when you use my own words against me," he murmured. Bending down, he took her chin with his, tilting her face back so he could kiss her nose. "Brat. What sort of tea?"

She grinned as he let her go.

Sunny's eyes were wide as she stared over at her. "You're so brave."

"Nah, his bark is worse than his bite."

"No, it's not," Sunny argued.

"It's definitely not," Brody said, sitting beside her. She leaned into him.

The Fox came over and poured them their tea. "There you go, ma'am. And for you, sir?" he asked Brody in a perfect British accent.

"It's weird when you call me sir." Brody shuddered.

The Fox grinned.

Duke walked into the room, looking shocked. Sunny jumped up, rattling the table.

"Duke? What is it?"

"I just went over and spoke to Sav," he said.

"What's wrong? Is it Livvy? Do I need to go over there?"

"No, baby. Best to stay here. The guy that pulled up in that truck. That was his brother, Cash."

"The one who disappeared? Who Sav thought had died?" Sunny asked.

"Yep. Turns out, he's not dead."

"Well," the Fox said. "That's a twist even I didn't see coming."

~

AN HOUR LATER, Brody closed his eyes as he rested his head against the headrest. After that announcement, none of them had really felt like playing. Sunny had made an effort, making them hot chocolate with whipped cream and sprinkles. It had been fun, but also, he was kind of relieved to be going home.

Autumn groaned in the backseat.

"What's wrong, Bunny?" the Fox asked.

"My tummy hurts."

"I think your hot chocolate was more sprinkles than anything else," Brody commented, twisting to rub her leg.

"Pup, sit back around. That's not safe. Baby girl, do you need me to pull over?"

"No. I'll be all right. That was weird, huh? That guy coming back from the dead, and on Christmas day," she mused.

"Yep, like a real Christmas miracle," Brody said.

"That's the sort of miracle I don't need," the Fox said as he drove them home.

Yeah, that would be more of a nightmare than a miracle.

Autumn suddenly gasped in the backseat. "Stop the car!"

The Fox slammed on the brakes and was out of the car before Brody could register what was going on.

The Fox opened Tutu's door. "What is it? Are you going to be ill?"

"No! Let me out! Let me out! It's snowing!"

Brody peered out the window. Whoa. It was light but it was definitely snowing.

"Hell, Bunny. You gave me a fright," the Fox scolded as he got her out of the car.

Brody climbed out as well, watching on with a grin as Tutu danced around, her hands out.

"That's so cute," the Fox commented.

"Come on, Brody-bear! Do a snow dance with me!"

With a laugh, Brody joined in as the Fox watched on with an indulgent smile.

Tutu threw her head back. "It's a snowy little Christmas after all!"

Half an hour later, the Fox bundled them back into the car, grumbling about them getting ill from being cold.

When they were in the garage, he helped Brody out of the

car before reaching into the back to pick up an exhausted Autumn, who slumped against him as he held her on his hip.

"It's a miracle," Tutu said, raising her head up to look at them both sleepily.

"The snow?" Brody asked. "That's not really a miracle in Montana."

"No, silly billy, that I found the two of you. And that's all I could ever want or need this year and every other. And maybe a *Tums*. My tummy is really hurting now."

"Come on, Pup, Bunny, time for bed. And a tummy rub. And if you're really good, I'll tell you the story of how the Fox got his very own happy ever after."

"That's my favorite story of all," Tutu replied.

His too.

Printed in Great Britain
by Amazon